BACKSTAGE WITH HER EX

BY
LOUISA GEORGE

MILLS &
BOON

First published in Great Britain 2013
by Mills & Boon, an imprint of Harlequin (UK) Limited,
Harlequin (UK) Limited, Eton House, 18-24 Paradise Road,
Richmond, Surrey TW9 1SR

© Louisa George 2013

ISBN: 978 0 263 91054 4

Harlequin (UK) policy is to use papers that are natural, renewable and recyclable products and made from wood grown in sustainable forests. The logging and manufacturing processes conform to the legal environmental regulations of the country of origin.

Printed and bound in Spain
by Blackprint CPI, Barcelona

She straightened her clothes, then turned slamming face to face with Nate.

He stared right back at her, his hand reaching out palm up in a question. 'Sasha? Sasha Snow...'

'Nathan—' She started to explain, but suddenly she was grabbed by his security guard, who shouted into a walkie-talkie. 'Now. Now. The car's leaving. Go, Nate. You want this one?'

This one? What was she? A toy? A groupie? 'Wait, no. You've got it wrong. I'm not—'

At that same moment, two more security guards burst into the room, grabbed her by the waist and ran her out through the corridor in a blur of clamouring, screaming women tearing at her hair, her clothes. The chant of *Nate. Nate. Nate*, ringing in her ears.

'Nathan… Wait—' Her voice mingled with the rest and got lost. Watching his leather-jacketed back disappear into a blacked-out limousine, she breathed out a sigh of irritation. That was that.

Damn. He was gone. A fleeting almost-reconciliation.

Then she felt someone touch the back of her head and push her into the plush car seat next to him. The door slammed closed.

And with a jerk they eased into the night-time London traffic to the accompaniment of bright flash photography. On the way to who knew where, with the ex she'd dumped and a whole lot of explaining to do.

Dear Reader,

I'm so thrilled to be part of the MODERN TEMPTED™ series! The stories in this exciting new line are everything I look for in a romance: sizzling sexual tension, a deeply emotional journey and lots of flirty fun along the way!

Nathan Munro, hero of this book, has had a lot of fun—almost too much—since he ran out on his first love, Sasha Sweet, a decade ago. But when she falls back into his life, he is forced to examine his actions, his past and, ultimately, his future.

Sasha, however, is reluctant to fall for Nathan's legendary rock-star charm. She has her sights firmly set on Mr Boring but Safe, if only she could find him. So Nate has his work cut out to convince her that Mr Very Wrong could possibly become Mr Very Right.

The settings for this book are two places where I've had a lot of fun: amazing Tuscany, rich with history, fabulous food and delicious wine, and London. What could be more exhilarating than the pulse of such a vibrant, sophisticated city? It's a fabulous place to fall in love (trust me, I know!).

I hope you enjoy reading Nate and Sasha's story! Look out for Cassie's story in the second book of the Sweet Sisters duet. Coming soon!

Louisa x

For all my writing news and release dates, visit me at www.LouisaGeorge.com.

Having tried a variety of careers in retail, marketing and nursing (where a scratchy starched uniform was mandatory), **Louisa George** is now thrilled that her dream job of writing for Mills & Boon means she gets to go to work in her pyjamas.

Originally from Yorkshire, England, Louisa now lives in Auckland, New Zealand, with her husband, two sports-mad teenage sons and two male cats. Writing romance is her opportunity to covertly inject a hefty dose of pink into her heavily testosterone-dominated household.

When she's not writing or reading Louisa loves to spend time with her family and friends, enjoys travelling and adores eating great food (preferably cooked by someone else). She's also hopelessly addicted to zumba.

Visit her at www.louisageorge.com.

I've been very lucky to have made some amazing friends over the years—some older, some younger, some wiser and some…not so (but we had a lot of laughs getting wise, usually after the event!). You know who you are—and if you're wondering… *does she mean me?* Yes, I do.

This book is dedicated to you all with heartfelt thanks for the wild ride, and lots of love xxx

CHAPTER ONE

HIDING OUT IN the gents' toilets backstage at the London Arena was not one of Sasha Sweet's personal highs. VIP toilets they might have been but, gold taps be damned, she wanted to go home.

I'll kill you, Cassie.

Bad enough she'd let herself be harangued into this ridiculous exercise, but ducking into the men's room in a moment of rare claustrophobic panic? All kinds of embarrassing.

A whoosh of air and a wall of encroaching noise announced the arrival of someone else in the room. Thank God she'd found an empty cubicle.

She checked the state of the wall before she slumped against it. Grateful to be in an empty cubicle? In the men's room? *Could my life get any worse?*

She held her breath to listen, knowing if she was discovered in here, flouting all security rules, she'd never achieve what she'd set out to do. And the dreams of fourteen kids would literally go down the pan, along with her professional reputation.

Plan A should have worked just fine: approach someone in authority, ask politely, make an appointment. Not hide out like a weird stalker. *In a cubicle.* While thousands of fans charged the backstage corridors wanting a piece of the notoriously damaged, famously over-sexed rock deity, Nate Munro.

Where was Plan B when she needed it?

A deep American accent bounced off the tiled walls. 'Quick, Nate. In here. Give us five minutes 'til they've been herded out. There's a car on its way to pick you up out the back.'

No. Sasha's shoulders crept towards her jaw, tightening the muscles around her neck like a noose. Not Nate. Not here. Not in this bathroom.

'What happened to Security? They're crazy out there.' Sure enough, it was Nate's voice now, much deeper, richer than she remembered, but unmistakably his. Tinged with his working-class roots and a smattering of amusement, but refined by maturity and years of stateside living.

The American voice responded with an air of glee, 'Crazy for *you*. They love *you*. The world loves you, Nate. You are gold.'

True enough. Aeons ago in Sasha's smitten seventeen-year-old eyes being with him had felt as if she'd been sprinkled with gold dust. *Nathan Munro.* Her eyes fluttered closed at the storm of innocent memories. A young singer desperate to be heard. Night after night of listening to his songs, songs he'd written about her.

He'd scaled the heights against the odds. She'd watched his life spiral out of control, as Chesterton had turned its back on him. And she'd been as scathing as the rest.

But now… Wild boy turned out-of-control rock star. Sold out across the globe on his five continents Hall of Fame tour, catapulted to the top of the charts with his husky sultry songs and edgy dark style. The devil with a god's voice.

And powerful too. What he wanted he got and to hell with the consequences.

So what the heck she thought she'd achieve by asking

him for help now, she didn't know. But Sasha inhaled, renewing her resolve. It had been for ever ago. Ten years. He'd probably forgotten about her, about *them*. Or hated her, still.

No matter. She would find a way to ask him for help, and make good on that promise to her kids—that was what was important, not their past history. But she couldn't face him here, after all this time, not in a loo. Even she wouldn't be able to take herself seriously surrounded by pipe work and the cloying smell of pine.

No, she was a music professional and she had standards. She'd find another way: phone his agent, bribe him into submission. Beg. Something.

So just leave. Please.

The American spoke again. 'You want me to find you someone for tonight? There're plenty of women out there. Your usual? Blonde? Tall? Big—'

'Sure. Whatever.'

'I'll get the guys onto it.' The crackle of a walkie-talkie split the room.

'But only for an hour or so. I've got a date later and I don't want to be late.' Nate's voice was laced with irritation.

What? Sasha's shoulders hiked to her ears again. He was planning a one-nighter *and* a date?

Well, the man had stamina.

And no morals.

And that was none of her business.

She'd got over him a long time ago. Hard not to with his colourful love life splashed front page most days of the week. Supermodels, actresses, singers hung off his arm at every opportunity. She just hoped he wasn't planning on entertaining in here; she had things to do.

'So you're not going to the afterparty?' the American asked. 'Twelve months of non-stop touring and you're going on a date instead of getting loose? She must be special.'

'I'll come along to the party later.'

'So who is it this time? Not Cara again? She's trouble, you know. Two stints in rehab. Possession. You've got to steer clear from girls like that.'

'But she did my sales a heap of good. She was good value.'

'Nice thinking, Nate. Point well made. Keep your options open. A pretty lady on your arm keeps the rest of your fans hopeful. But remember, don't do anything stupid— stay away from the two cardinal sins: drugs and marriage. Drugs bring their own problems, pal, but cosy is the kiss of death to your career.'

'I had a lucky escape with that fiasco of an engagement. I'm never going there again.'

Sasha's frown deepened. Did she detect a tinge of boredom in his voice? Something not right in Nate's opulent successful world? And since when was marriage part of the axis of evil?

He'd clearly changed beyond anything she remembered. The Nathan she'd known at first had been sweet and kind and hadn't thought of women as good value. But then, she'd witnessed the beginning of that change: the way he'd morphed from sweet teenager to brooding, angry young man.

Seemed that downward trajectory hadn't stopped.

Suddenly the shrill blare of a text message made her jump.

Shoot! No. *No!* She clamped a hand to her mouth. Had she said that out loud?

Fumbling into her bag, she fell against the wall, dropped her phone and then watched in silent Slow… Motion… Horror. It bounced and slithered across the tiles, under the cubicle door, and out to the other side.

Crouching down, she watched, mortified, as her bright sparkly purple cell finally came to a stop next to a pair of battered black biker boots.

So yes, it seemed her life could get much worse.

Silence reverberated around the room for two long seconds, save for the hard thump of her heart against her ribs. And the shuffle of heavy feet.

'What have we got here?' The American voice deepened as a hand reached for her phone. He read the message out. *"Target located? Is he still to die for? What about that ass?"'* He laughed. 'Hey, Nate, either you've cornered the gay military market, or we have ourselves a desperate female admirer.'

Desperate?

A loud hammering on the cubicle door rocked into Sasha's body as a rash seeped through her skin, burning bright and hot. 'Hey. You. This is VIP access only…and the men's room. Get out here now before I call the cops.'

No, thanks. Standing in front of an assembly hall full of disenchanted teens was less terrifying than coming face to face with an ex like Nate.

If he remembered the way things had ended between them he definitely wouldn't want to answer her cry for help, but she had to try. She couldn't face the kids on Monday and say she hadn't asked him. In reality, this could be her only chance and it wasn't as if she had any sentimental feelings for him—time had certainly filled that well. Finding her courage again, she inhaled. Maybe asking him in a loo wouldn't be so…degrading.

So be a grown-up. Steadying herself, Sasha pulled back the lock. Sometimes, being a grown-up sucked.

Before she could speak the door slammed open and a blur of dark suit brushed against her, jamming her arm behind her back and her cheek against the wall. He patted her hands, her pockets and legs. The voice in her ear was hard and unforgiving. 'There you go, darling. Take it easy.'

'Let go of me. Let go now. Or *I* call the cops. Harassment. Assault.'

'She's clean.'

'Of course I'm clean. What is this?'

'Can't be too careful, ma'am. We meet all sorts of weir-does in this business.'

'And that's just the people who work in it, right?' Shoving out of the bear's hold, she straightened her clothes then turned, slamming body-to-body with Nate.

His jaw tensed, and his stare deepened as he took her in, recognition clearly filtering through his brain as he swept his glance up and down her body.

In response she froze, unable to take her eyes from him. Sure, she'd seen the pictures, had some old grainy ones of her own, she'd even stolen quick glances at the rock magazines' centre spreads, heck she'd just watched him perform two hours of perfect harmonies and slow sexy dance moves in the final concert of his tour. But nothing had prepared her for the real thing up close.

He seemed taller, definitely broader, not the teenager she'd once fallen in love with. He was one hundred per cent man. All sex, with his wavy chocolate-coloured hair dipping lazily to one side. She remembered the soft just-washed feel of it, the faint scent of apples.

Her gaze ran across his face, past those famous soft-caramel eyes, the refined cheeks peppered with his trade-mark stubble, the perfect curve of his lips.

But she couldn't stop there. After all, he'd always been a feast to her senses. She imagined the ruffled feel of his shirt, and the hard muscle underneath. His smell of leather and man. Remembered the long legs for ever encased in black denim, rough against her juvenile skin. The arrogant stance that told the world he didn't give a damn, when she knew he'd cared deeply. Deeply enough to be hurt by the rejection, to leave town altogether and never look back.

And yes, thank you, Cassie, his ass was still to die for.

He stared right back at her, stepping back, palm up in a question. 'Sasha? Sasha Sweet?'

'Nathan—' She started to explain, but suddenly she was grabbed by the bear, who shouted into his walkie-talkie, 'Now. Now. The car's leaving. Go, Nate. You want this one too?'

This one? What was she? A toy? A groupie? 'Wait, no. You've got it wrong. I'm not—'

'No?' The minder grinned and shook his head. 'Had a change of heart, sweetheart? There's plenty more who'd take your place.'

Oh, merry hell. The bear really did think she was a groupie. Nate must have muttered something, or nodded, and she'd missed it before he disappeared into the melee outside.

But at that same moment two more security guards burst into the room, grabbed her by the waist and ran her out through the corridor in a blur of clamouring, screaming women tearing at her hair, her clothes. The chant of *Nate, Nate,* Nate, ringing in her ears.

'Nathan…Wait—' Her voice mingled with the rest, and got lost. Watching his leather-jacketed back disappear into a blacked-out limousine, she breathed out a hiss of irritation. That was that.

He was gone. And now no result for the school; she should have found her nerve and asked him.

Then she felt someone touch the back of her head and push her into the plush car seat opposite Nathan.

He slowly leaned back and grinned, almost oblivious to the two giggling peroxided semi-naked women who had draped themselves over him and now appeared to be cleaning out his ears—*with their tongues.* The door slammed closed.

And with a jerk the car eased towards the arena exit to the accompaniment of bright flash photography. On the way to who knew where, with the ex she dumped, an audience of twin pipe-cleaners on legs, and a whole lot of explaining to do.

CHAPTER TWO

WELL, WELL. THIS was interesting. Ten years in the business and Nate had had a lot of surprises. Some good. Some not so. Some pretty painful and costly. But a flame-haired ex with a penchant for kicking first and asking questions—er, never…wasn't one of them. Until now.

He watched her struggle with the every-day reality of his chaotic life on the road, her shock at the girls in the car. Meanwhile some weird emotion played Dixie with his gut. Was he pleased to see her? That, he hadn't had time to compute.

But images of the last time he saw her flickered through his brain like a bad black and white film. Rain. Tears. Hurt. A big fist of anger that had lodged in his chest, and taken months to shake.

But it was all a long time and countless liaisons ago. He couldn't remember the last time he'd given her any thought at all.

Waving a hand to the girls to let up, he leaned forward. 'Hello, Sasha. To what do I owe this…pleasure?'

'Where exactly are you taking me? I need to get out. To my sister. She's waiting for me back at the arena.' Shaking her mane of soft red curls, she frowned, her lipstick-tinged mouth forming the pout that swung him back through the years. The punch to his chest was surprising. 'That bear of a thug, your security guy, he thought…I don't want…you know. I'm not a…groupie.' Her eyes narrowed even more as she glanced towards the girls.

And for a second he felt a strange ping of shame. Fleeting. Then gone. After all, Sasha's betrayal had been one of the reasons he'd moved on in life anyway. And boy, was life good now. 'But you used to be my groupie, Sasha. And, if I remember rightly, you used to like it.'

Although back then sex had been a solemn promise for the future, not a reality.

At her quick blink he felt the laugh rumble up from his chest, heard the high-pitched giggles from the girls against his neck. Sasha didn't crack a smile.

Okay. So this was clearly going to be important. Or why else was she here?

He tapped on the window for the driver to pull over, slapped each of the girls on the backside and let them out into the following entourage cars.

Meanwhile Sasha shook her head in that way schoolteachers did when you disappointed them. He recognised it because he'd experienced it often enough. 'And just like that they disappear. Everyone does exactly what Nate Munro says?'

He shrugged. 'Sure. I thought you'd prefer to do this… whatever it is…in private. Just you and me. Unless you're into threesom—'

'No!'

'Relax, Sasha. It was a joke.' She was too easy to wind up. 'I don't want to get naked with you either.'

Liar. Post-show sex was as habitual as coffee in the mornings. And right now her navy-blue eyes and feisty spirit sparked the right amount of interest. He watched in amusement as she gripped the strap on her bag. No wedding ring. Interesting. Still, that meant little these days. And why had he looked at her fingers?

A purely male instinctive reaction. Right?

But everything he remembered about Sasha Sweet was laced with regret. Not just the one that got away, she was the one who had stamped hard on his heart.

'Now I know everything the papers say is true. You're just a good-time guy. Shallow. Over-sexed...'

'Oh? You've been reading up about me?' Stretching out his legs across the lush thick white carpet, he grinned, slow and lazy so she'd understand just how good his life had been. After her. 'Believe me, it's been infinitely better than anything they print.'

'I have not been reading up about you.' She rolled her eyes. 'I just happened to notice some headline about your crazy life in the States. It's certainly a far cry from Chesterton.'

'And then some.' He shuddered at the mention of the place that had cut ties with him. That had branded him with the same tarnish they had his no-hope father. A hooligan, out of control. Bad to the bone. And no one, not even Sasha, had ever come to his defence.

'Leaving Chesterton was the best thing I ever did. And yes, there are some mad parties in LA. It comes with the territory.' The press had wasted no time covering the best bits—it just happened the best bits were also the worst. Drunk and debauched had been one hell of a ride.

She tugged at his arm. 'Nate, I need to—'

'I know. Here.' He felt in his pocket for her phone. 'Text her back. I presume the Cassie ID refers to your little sister?'

She looked surprised. 'Yes. Of course. You remember Cassie? Although, she's not so little these days, at twenty-five.'

'How could I ever forget the infamous Sweet sisters?'

Even though he'd long since put their failed relationship down to innocent first-love infatuation, he hadn't forgotten the details. Three feisty red-headed girls who had set the fragile hearts of every nubile boy in Chesterton racing. With Sasha, the middle sister, the only woman who'd ever said no to him.

And here she was, all grown-up and seriously hot.

The freckles he'd loved to count and kiss way back in the Dark Ages were still there on her fresh lightly made-up face. Her spirit, clearly, hadn't diminished. Neither had the curves highlighted by the tight capri trousers and dark mesh top, making her look as if she'd just walked out of a fifties' movie set, or the translucent skin that had sent shivers down his adolescent spine. But he'd got steel in there now.

Working in a business of backstabbing and greed, he was used to people trying to piggy-back on his success. He'd been taken for a ride too many times to count and wouldn't be doing it again; a costly separation had taught him that lesson.

So why his interest was piqued by this particular old girlfriend he didn't know. He might as well just get the cheque book out now. Far easier than going through a messy conversation.

Grabbing the glittery phone from his outstretched hand, she glanced at the screen and visibly cringed. 'I'm sorry about that. Cassie might be an adult, but she hasn't fully grown up yet.'

'And what are you going to reply to her?'

'Oh…I don't know.' She looked up through thick dark eyelashes, her lips pursed, teasingly. 'That you're still obnoxious and full of yourself.'

'And with an ass to die for?'

'See? Obnoxious.' She flashed a smile, which did something funny to his heart. He put it down to being on the road for too long.

'I aim to please. And it seems to work for the most part. I have to admit, you surprise me, Sasha. I never thought you'd do something like this. You always played everything so safe.' He returned the smile with one of his own as he undid the top button on his shirt, ready to have a little fun.

Instead of the flustered reaction he'd imagined, she sat forward and pinned him to the seat with an ice-cool gaze. 'I did not.'

'Yeah? Grade-A student, always toed the line. Never broke the rules—at least never broke them for me. So what's changed? Why are you in my car en route to a fancy hotel?'

'Hotel? Oh, for goodness' sake, get over yourself.' She blinked quickly, the cool fading into fluster. 'I...I said, I'm not here for sex.'

'Oh, yes, and I remember you saying that before too. But I never did quite believe you.' He leaned forward, met her almost in the middle of the seat, caught a glimpse of fire in her eyes before she turned away.

She'd been saving herself for when they were married or some such foolish idea. At least, until they were engaged. He wondered, fleetingly, who had taken his place, been her first time.

He shook that thought away along with the accompanying uninvited tension that zipped through his veins. And fought back an urge to run his fingers through a curl, see if it was as soft as he remembered. 'Your body always did give you away.'

'Not any more. I have full control.'

'Really?' He focused on her legs, did a slow journey up to her breasts, her throat, her mouth. Awareness crackled around the car sucking out the oxygen. After five long seconds he met her gaze. 'You want to put it to the test?'

'Absolutely not. You should save your energy for someone who'd be more...grateful. Like the poor misguided gruesome twosome you just had in here.' She glared at him. But he didn't miss the flash of heat in her eyes. 'Look, this has been a mistake.'

And the blushing was still the same; she never could control that. A full peachy rash bloomed in her cheeks, spread to her neck and disappeared into that midnight-blue top.

Dragging his eyes away from her, he tried to breathe out the weird emotions thrumming in his chest.

Outside, the city lights illuminated Marble Arch, traffic slowed even at this time of night.

London.

For the first time in years, he was back home. At least it used to be. Home now was a sprawling Malibu mansion overlooking the ocean. But sometimes he missed the vibrancy of this city, the exciting pulse that emanated from the streets and throbbed through his veins, mixing with the comforting feel of the familiar.

Or was that just his strange reaction at seeing Sasha Sweet again?

She looked out of the window, too, for a few moments until her surprisingly girly phone signalled a new message. When she'd finished reading she tilted her head in his direction. 'Can you drop me off now? Cassie's going to meet me. I'll get the tube from here.'

'Are you serious? You used to cling to me on the tube. You hated it—all those crowds, all that danger hidden in dark corners. The rush of hot air. The noise. Rats.'

'Well, looky here, things move on. I have.'

'Clearly. If you're sure.' He tapped on the screen to alert his driver, then turned back to face her, still confused as to why she was here and why his body was so stirred up by her. 'But what's going on, Sasha? We both know this isn't about my backside or any kind of sexual intent. "Target located," Cassie said. Why am I your target? What do you want?'

'It doesn't matter. Seriously, forget it. All this…' She gestured to the car, to the unopened bottles of champagne in the console. 'You're way too busy, and…different from how I remembered.'

'I hope so.'

'I didn't mean it was a good thing.'

'Champagne is always a good thing. As is success.' In truth, he didn't have time for another sob story. He already had sacks full of begging letters at his manager's office.

But her eyes drew his gaze and he was fixed there with a strange need to prove he could do something she hadn't— listen. 'Okay. I'm probably going to regret this, but I've got five minutes. Try me.'

As the car drew to a halt he watched her take a slow deep breath then exhale the way they'd all been taught back in form four music class. Sing on the out-breath. So he knew if she needed to keep her voice steady it was something important.

'I'm a teacher now, Nate. Music. And my show choir has reached the finals of a national contest. Problem is, we can't afford the fares up to Manchester, the hotel costs, costumes and everything. We need your help.'

As he'd thought. Just someone else asking for a hand-out. Disappointing. 'You want a cheque? Cash? We could stop by a cash machine.'

'No. Part of the contest is about raising the money, not just digging deep into our own pockets—not that we could if we wanted to. It's all about the process—teaching the children about community spirit and involvement, you know the kind of thing. You don't get handouts, you need to work hard to achieve…' As she spoke about the project her eyes blazed with a mesmerising fervour.

Immediately he was thrown back to a time when they'd had their future ahead of them, when they'd believed they could do anything. Be anything they dreamed of. Together. He remembered getting lost in her excitement, in that thick luscious hair, in her. Until the day that fervour in her eyes had mingled with disappointment and distrust.

'We thought about holding a concert at the school to get some funds, but few people around our neighbourhood could afford to come even if they wanted to. No one wants to pay to see a bunch of kids singing and dancing, not...' she fixed him with hopeful eyes '—unless we had a guest star. That would raise a lot of interest from everywhere else too, and, bingo, we get our much-needed cash. I figured we could pay you a fee out of the door money, fifty-fifty.'

He laughed. Loudly. 'A fee? You have to be joking. You couldn't afford me in a million light years.'

'Yes, well, like I said, coming here was a mistake. Why would you want to help us? There was a time when you'd have done this kind of thing for free but I guess we're too late.'

'About a decade or so.' So that was that—he was off the hook from her crazy idea. But one thing niggled him. 'And you stowed away in the men's toilet just to ask me this?'

'I did not stow. Stowing is not my style. It was an accident.'

'Sasha, no one accidentally finds themselves in the men's room. Come on, if you want me to help you, you have to at least be honest.'

She shrugged. 'A friend of Cassie's got me backstage, but I wasn't sure how you'd react at seeing me again, and then when all those fans broke through the barrier and surged down the corridor I thought I was going to get crushed. I panicked.'

'And then played jack-in-the-box in the loo? To be honest I'd have preferred you jumping out of a cake semi-naked, or something.' Now that was an entertaining thought. He'd gone from never thinking about her at all, to imagining her half dressed. How did that work? 'You always did like to make a show of things.'

'I did not.'

'No? Remember that night you borrowed your sister's

new bra and padded it with tissues to see if I'd notice—' He laughed as his hands curved in front of his chest. 'I noticed.'

She clearly did remember if the new flush on her cheeks was anything to go by, and how he'd told her she was perfect without any trimmings or falseness. Their last night. When they'd almost lost control of their agreed celibacy.

Their heated innocent fumblings swarmed back in a cloud of memories. He'd needed her, needed a release, an escape from the realities of his life. And they'd been so close to sealing their love.

Low in his abdomen something tightened and prickled hot. The jolt of his body's response jarred. He so wasn't in the mood for a trip down Memory Lane or the unwelcome feelings she invoked. In his experience women were trouble, particularly exes. 'Why all the cloak and dagger stuff? Why didn't you just get hold of my manager?'

'Oh duh. Why didn't I think of that?' She smacked the palm of her hand against her forehead. 'You, Mr Out of Touch with Reality, have no idea how hard that is. We tried calling, letters, emails. The kids even sent in a video. But nothing. No reply from your office. And now the deadline's looming.'

'I see. So desperate measures, eh?' That tingling zipped through his body again. He liked the idea of Sasha desperate. Images of her youthful body lashed against his mixed with the full-woman curves in front of him now. One thing was for sure: she'd always had an effect on him.

God, he needed to get laid. Soon. And not with her, because he never did reruns of his mistakes.

Which was why his indignation grew as he watched her scrape her hair back into an untidy ponytail, with a hair tie she kept on her wrist, not caring how she looked. He couldn't help watching her, unable to remember the last time he'd been in the same room as a woman who hadn't continually looked in a mirror or asked for reassurance about her appearance. Sasha was a breath of fresh air in his world of fakery, but she was trading on their past and that hurt.

'London is awash with Z-list celebrities desperate to raise their profiles. Why not ask one of them? Why me?' He didn't know what he wanted her to reply. That she'd never stopped thinking of him? That this was a way of connecting with him again?

'Aside from the fact you're the only successful person I know, or that came out of Chesterton High?'

'And that was despite it. Did you think I'd be an easy target? Or is it because of our history?'

'I wouldn't use that, Nate.'

'Isn't that exactly what you're doing?'

He watched as she struggled to maintain calm. 'No. I didn't want to dredge up the past, but somehow Cassie managed to convince me to try to get hold of you. This is all about helping the kids out. They don't know about what happened between us—very few people do. What we had was…well, I guess it was special. It was private.'

'So special you refused to hear my explanation. So special you turned your back like everyone else. So damned special you couldn't even look me in the eye.' But he'd looked into hers. Right when he'd willed her to speak up for him, to serve as character witness or do something to save him, the way he'd have done anything for her.

She gripped the door handle. 'You hit someone, Nathan. You told me you had. I wasn't going to lie and say you hadn't. The police were hammering on the door screaming that you'd had to be hauled off the poor kid before you killed him. You were all shouting. I was seventeen and scared as hell by the aggression—from you all. I wouldn't have been heard even if I'd wanted to.'

Which she hadn't. He hadn't told her why he'd hit Craig.

Why he couldn't stop. She'd noticed his raw knuckles and he'd told her just enough to stop her asking questions.

But ancient history didn't matter; he'd put it so far behind him he could barely remember it.

So why the tightening in his chest?

He shook his head. 'Just forget it.'

'You always were trouble, Nathan Munro, and don't deny it.' Her lips stretched into an upwards curl. She might well have developed into a stunning ardent woman, but the smile was still very youthful, teasing. 'And it looks like you still are.'

'I try my best.' Trouble, and never good enough for her and her family. Even in a rundown place like Chesterton there'd been a pecking order and his family had been at the bottom.

But okay, she'd never sold him out to the press, though many others had.

Bond Street tube station lights flickered directly outside, but she made no effort to get out of the car. Tapping his fingers on the leather seat, he waited for her to leave; he had no intention of spending time again with Sasha. Some things were just best left alone—memories, for a start, trampled hearts. Their lost past. 'And?'

'And…' Her mouth tightened into a thin line as anxiety flitted across her eyes. 'The school I work at? It's Chesterton High.'

Un-frickin-believable.

He'd put all this behind him and had no desire to go back there again. For any of them, least of all her.

'So let me get this right. In the precious amount of spare time I have, you want me to drop everything to help you, and help that school too, after all that happened?'

Her eyes widened, her chin tilted higher, daring him to agree to her ridiculous suggestion. 'Yes.'

'Not a chance, sweet thing.'

She gasped. Using the nickname he'd called her throughout their two-year relationship seemed to strike a chord. Her mouth fell open as if she was about to say something, then she closed it.

He leaned across her, careful not to brush against that hair, or those curves, caught the handle of the car and opened the door. 'I'm sorry. This crazy plan of yours won't be happening. You can go now.'

'Wait.' Pausing with one foot on the pavement and the other in the car, she tilted her head to him. 'There is another reason I thought you might want to help us.'

'I can't wait for this. What could possibly be more compelling than what you've suggested so far?'

Her discomfort was palpable, her eyes turbulent with emotion. Now the words tumbled out in a rush as she dragged in a breath. 'It's a mixed ability choir…called No Limits.'

The ache in his chest was swift and sudden, finding all the empty places and filling them. Disarmed by her words, and the way she looked at him with empathy and sadness, he was thrown off kilter. 'You really know how to turn the screw, don't you, Sasha? You think I'd want to help because of my brother?'

'Marshall loved singing and dancing, Nate. And he loved being in the school choir.'

Marshall had loved Sasha, too, almost as much as Nate had. But he'd hated the school. He'd hated the bullies that ruined his life. And Nate's, for a while. But revenge was sweet when it came wrapped in international stardom.

And then…the ache deepened in wave after wave of pain. None of his success would bring Marshall back. 'So now you're using Marshall as collateral? Are there no limits to the lengths to which you'll stoop?'

'I just thought it might make a difference to you.' She'd

never treated Marshall as different, and he knew she'd have been as devastated as he was when Marshall died. At least, he assumed she knew of his death even though he'd tried to keep it quiet. But the furore afterwards as he'd lost control had been splashed over the newspapers.

'But this?'

'You wanted me to be honest, so hear me out. The kids in the choir are just like him. Excited, hopeful…special. They want to go to the national competition and be part of something that's normal. And they've got a good chance of placing too. They just need a break.'

'And me as a draw card.'

This was a game-changer. But he didn't know if he could walk into a room full of kids like Marshall and not make a fool of himself by losing it. He'd ploughed thousands of dollars into research, donated anonymously to charities, but he was scared about coming face to face with a kid like his brother.

'I never pegged you as a coward, Nate.'

'I'm not a coward.' Irritation tripped down his spine mixing with the other emotions she'd dredged up in him. 'I just don't need to go back there. I have nothing to prove.'

The laugh gushing from her throat was filled with passion. 'Oh, yeah? The Nathan Munro I knew always had something to prove. You've spent the last ten years showing the world how good you can be despite your upbringing. But right now the only thing you're proving is how much you've changed. And not for the better.'

Retrieving a card from her purse, she regained her composure. Which was a shame, because something about her all fired up connected with something deep in him. 'If, by any kind of miracle, you change your mind here's my contact details. And the school—well, you know where that is. Please just think about.'

He didn't need to. He wasn't doing it.

Crumpling the card into his fist, he frowned. 'Sasha, I could find that school with my eyes closed. I just don't want to.'

'That's okay. I understand. It was worth a try, though, eh?' She pressed her lips together and shrugged. 'Good to see you after all this time.'

'Yeah, sure.' Was it? He didn't know. But one thing he was sure of: he didn't want to see that school or her again. He just didn't trust her or the weird and immediate effect she had on him.

Then she dashed out of the door and into the tube station. Leaving him with a distinct unease, accompanied by a determination not to let Sasha Sweet get to him.

But as he looked at the tatty bit of cardboard with her name on it, he got the feeling that was going to be very hard to do.

CHAPTER THREE

'WHAT IS IT with men?' Sasha slumped into the deep cushions on her lumpy old sofa and shook her head. 'I'll never understand them.'

'What you really mean is, what is it with Nate Munro?' Cassie came through from the kitchenette, bearing mugs of thick creamy hot chocolate topped with marshmallows, and snuggled in next to her. Mainly because in Sasha's cramped flat there was just no space for another piece of furniture.

'Aaaargh. He's so annoying.' And so was her body's reaction to him.

'I can't believe you rode in his limo, you lucky thing. I bet it was amazing.'

'It wasn't like I had a choice. It was tantamount to kidnapping. And I wasn't looking at the interior décor.' Technically she'd been tagged as a desperate groupie and bundled in like a piece of merchandise. But she doubted that would make it seem less glamorous in Cassie's eyes.

Inhaling the chocolate aroma, Sasha tried to instill calm. Nothing was ever so bad that chocolate couldn't help. Except…she breathed in again…nothing changed. Her pulse still jittered, her head pounded, and every time she closed her eyes she could see his lazy smile. Only instead of feeling angry with him she felt flustered and breathless and strangely confused. First time ever the chocolate magic hadn't worked.

Cassie nudged her. 'You can hardly blame him, sis, you knew he'd never come through. He's too famous, too busy. Too darned hot to care about a school he was expelled from or an ex from years back.'

Hot for sure. Yes, yes, Sasha knew that, and she hated to admit it. Since the second she'd laid eyes on him again she'd been fighting to keep her hormones under control. And failing.

It had always been the same with him; he had a way of making her whole body light up with a touch. After he'd gone she'd thrown herself into forgetting him, and that had worked just fine. Until now.

'And you can stop with the sighing too, Cassie. He might be beautiful, but he's not kind if he can turn my lovely choir down like that. He's selfish and brooding and...' She stopped right there. Thoughts straying in his direction were not good for her mental health.

'And you really are hooked on finding someone kind, aren't you? You're a lost cause.' Cassie giggled. 'Top of my list comes abs, eyes...ass. Rich helps. Sense of humour, definitely—'

Sasha sighed, grateful for Cassie's never-ending sense of optimism and fun. Grateful too, that, with Suzy's help, Sasha had shielded their adorable little sister from the fall-out of their father's death. At least one of the three sisters had survived intact.

'I just can't see me falling for anyone who doesn't treat me as an equal. I want to feel safe, and cherished. I don't want to live on an edge or spend my life worrying whether he loves me or not. I want boring. Old tatty slippers and cardigans. Holding hands for our sixtieth wedding anniversary like Granny and Gramps.'

After her father had died all ideas of being safe either emotionally or financially were ripped apart, leaving the whole family bereft. She didn't want to invite more hurt into her life and the few less-than-successful experiences she'd had with men had proved her right. Loving someone could be unpredictable, based on lies that hurt like hell.

So when her Prince Charming arrived, he'd be driving a Volvo and wearing sensible brogues.

Immediately, her thoughts strayed to slim long legs and big biker boots, tiled toilet floors and flashy limousines.

She shuddered. Way too dangerous.

'I know…' Cassie sat up and squished her left leg underneath her bottom, eyes firing with excitement. 'Do you want me to get Nate arrested? Then we can *convince* him to do it. Pat's a great policeman—I'm sure he'd find something on him.'

Sasha eyed Cassie in the way only a big sister could—a look that said *I love you, now shut up* at the same time. 'Will you stop with that? Ever since you started dating Pat the Plod you've been offering for him to arrest someone.'

'I know. I can't help it—the thought of him being all masculine and strong—ooh.' Cassie clasped her mug to her chest and sighed. 'Divine.'

'Just as I thought, it has more to do with the idea of handcuffs than an inflated sense of civic duty.' Sasha laughed and shook her head. 'But if the papers are to be believed Nate's been arrested way too many times already.'

'I'm sure they make half of that stuff up.'

'I dare say.' But the one time it had mattered—the first time—she'd let him go.

No—she'd turned her back on him like the rest. And with due cause. The man had attacked someone and she'd had enough violence in her life to put up with it from a boyfriend too. Seeing Nathan's aggressive reaction had sparked a deeply buried memory that she couldn't bear to relive. So she'd walked away.

'It's probably a good thing, anyway. I just have to work out a Plan B for the choir. Leave it with me…' She thought for a moment and came up with...precisely nothing. 'Okay, arresting him suddenly seems very attractive. Especially if I get to read him his rights...'

Tinny music jolted her attention.

Her mobile.

Knots tightened in her stomach as she relived the moment it slithered across the toilet tiles; the wretched thing had got her into too much trouble already tonight. She checked the number. No one she knew.

Cassie leaned over her shoulder and eyeballed the display. 'Answer it.'

'No. It's way past midnight. Who'd ring at this time? It'll be a crank.'

'Answer the darned thing. Or...I will.' Cassie grabbed for it. Sasha jumped off the sofa and stared at the unfamiliar number.

No way was she taking a chance on her flirtatious little sister nudging in on the act. If it was Nate Munro she needed to be professional and responsible, remember that this was about the choir, and not about herself, or her drumming heart rate. Probably a wrong number anyway. 'Hello?'

'Hey, sweet thing, is that you?'

'Once was funny, now it's just irritating. Stop calling me that.' Hearing the pet name she'd loved hit her hard in the gut. After ten years of honing her career into shape she was so far from being a sweet thing it was laughable. So, occasionally she allowed the pupils to think they'd got the better of her just so they'd see her as human and approachable. But she was always in control. Always.

But there was her body reacting all by itself again. The drumming developed into full-on bongos in her chest, her hands grew sticky and her peripheral vision fuzzied.

But her head was in full control. 'I thought you were on a date? What's the problem—couldn't she keep up with your ego, or the delightful twins' bimbo competition?'

A deep rumble permeated down the phone. 'Date? Oh, yes. That. It was great.'

'Didn't last long. Don't tell me, you peaked too soon.'

'Sweet thing, believe me, I haven't even started.' His voice lowered to a growl that sounded a lot like sex, and he knew damned well he was winding her up. 'You know, you show way more spirit over the phone than in person. Easy when you can't see me, eh? But don't forget I know how easy it is to make you blush.'

Too right. On cue heat swept across her cheeks and down her neck as if proving his point. Maybe her cocky attitude would ruin their chances, but somehow she didn't think so. She guessed he had his fair share of yes-people in his life. But Nate wouldn't like that. He liked down-to-earth honesty and playfulness rather than false praise. At least he used to. 'And you called because?' She crossed her fingers and prayed.

'I've been thinking.'

'Gosh, well done.'

'See? Spirit. I'd forgotten that.' His laugh was gentle and surprising. 'About your project. You want to give me more details? Dates, times…'

Hope rose as the drumming beat faster in off-beat demi-semi quavers. That hurt. 'So you'll do it? You'll do the concert?'

In answer to Sasha's thumbs-up sign and broad grin, Cassie gyrated across the floor, wiggling her skinny backside in an attempt to mimic Nate's very sexy stage performance.

Sasha held her breath and tried to control the relieved laughter. 'Thank you. Thank you so much—you don't know how much this means to the choir—'

'Hold on, Sasha, I'm not making any promises. I need to check my schedule. Text your address to this number and I'll send a car for you tomorrow at seven p.m. You can come to my hotel and we'll talk more.'

'Not that it doesn't sound fancy, and I'm very grateful, but I've been making my own way around London for years.' She didn't need any more reasons to be beholden to him. 'Just tell me where you're staying. I'll get there.'

'No.' He clearly didn't trust her with that kind of information. Not surprising really after she'd turned her back on him. At the time she'd called it self-preservation but, in hindsight, he'd probably seen it as betrayal. 'My car will be there at seven. Be ready.'

'But…'

'Sasha, this works better for me. I don't want anyone getting wind of this yet, okay? And the press have a way of finding things out.'

'And being nice interferes with your bad-boy image?'

'Really? You think I care what the press think? It's way too late for that. I don't want to get the kids' hopes up and then not be able to follow through. And it's my private cellphone, so don't ever give this number to anyone.'

Normally she didn't take kindly to being bossed around, but the guy had just given her an opening. The choir would be thrilled, their financial problems solved, if she could pull it off. And keep her jumping heart out of it. 'Okay. Seven p.m. tomorrow, then.'

'Oh, and one last thing, Sasha. This is just for Marshall, okay?'

'Mr Munro will see you now.' The bear appeared in the reception of the Grand Riverview Hotel, complete with earpiece and grimace. 'This way.'

'Nice to see a familiar face,' Sasha breathed as she struggled to keep up along the elegant corridor.

Velvet-embossed wallpaper in golden hues served as a backdrop to nineteen-twenties-style furniture. Petite bronze statuettes of dancers flanked the walls. *The price of one of those would pay for the whole choir to fly to Manchester, first class.* She was so out of her league, and then some. But, fingers clutching her briefcase, she determined to meet Nathan face to face as a music professional.

'We get a lot of familiar faces here, sweetheart, for a day or two.' Giving her just enough time to process the ramifications of that statement, the bear opened the door.

You're nothing special, his feigned smile said as he looked her up and down. Standing aside to let her in, he bowed lightly, muttering, 'Don't get too comfortable.'

Like that would happen. Especially with Mr Warm and Fuzzy here.

She blinked once, twice, not knowing what was more impressive: the expansive suite with panoramic views across London, or the fact that Nate was in it, looking extremely comfortable, standing by the bar. Looking extremely gorgeous too. Relaxed and confident. In control of everything: his staff, his surroundings, his emotions.

He'd grown in a way she hadn't. At least she didn't see herself like that—uber confident and all grown-up—even though she tried to be. He'd probably honed it from absorbing the adoration of thousands of fans, from years of live performances where self-belief was mandatory.

But regardless of the man he was now she knew his essence, where he'd come from, what he was truly like—the good, the bad and the downright ugly.

And yet, despite knowing what he was capable of, he was still strangely compelling to be with. Walking leisurely towards her, he smiled. Slim black jeans hung from slender hips, a black faded T-shirt hugged his toned frame.

She didn't have to guess what was under that T because she'd seen it over the years in the music press, smoky black and white images of Nate in various stages of undress, on CD covers that bordered on X-rated. She knew all about the sun-kissed carved abs, the thin line of dark hair… Her mouth dried.

She jerked her head upwards. Big mistake.

The moment she met his caramel-coated gaze her courage faltered. Why did he have to be so beautiful?

Was it appropriate to walk over and kiss him on the cheek? Shake hands? But he saved her the worry by stepping into her space and placing a warm cheek against hers. His lips grazed her skin sending ripples of heat through her veins.

'Sasha. Thanks for coming.'

'Thank you…too.' *Excellent. Excellent start. Not.*

And then the room seemed to press in as his familiar scent washed over her. This was the kind of place he was used to now. So far from the tiny council-flat bedroom he'd shared with Marshall, littered with guitars and sheet music, posters on the wall of his favourite damaged rock heroes. And a photograph of her by his bed.

Her throat filled. So many things she'd pushed to the back of her mind, or had simply forgotten. The honest sweetness of their first date. Their innocent journey to first love.

And now this. Such abject luxury, no wonder he'd offered to write her a cheque without missing a heartbeat. But could high living change a man? Could it tame him?

She'd read about his wild parties in Ibiza, the spats with paparazzi, riding his motorbike through a hotel reception. She guessed that really he was still the same man underneath the wealth.

Leading her to a couch that would never fit into the whole of her flat, even if she knocked the walls down, he held a glass of beer and offered her a flute of champagne. 'Drink?'

'Thanks. Nice place.' She raised her eyebrows and gestured to the door. 'Shame about the company you keep, though. Do you pay him to be rude?'

'Dario?' Nate's smile spread slowly across his lips, reached his eyes, which softened with genuine warmth. 'Only to my friends.'

She laughed. 'God help your enemies, then. I dread to think what you do to them.'

His gaze hardened from toffee to troubled. The hand holding his glass fisted and she thought for a second it might smash.

Brilliant. Bring up the past, why don't you?

He'd never explained why he'd launched the attack that had landed Craig in Intensive Care and she doubted he would now. And even more, it was still none of her business.

The silence that followed was mortifying. She watched as he regained control, softened the tight jawline, turned his back on her and walked to the window. 'You'd better tell me what you need me to do.'

Renewing her purpose, she deposited her flute on the glass coffee table and fished her folders from her well-loved leather messenger bag. She met his authority with her own. 'I have spreadsheets here with a projected timetable, financial forecast, health and safety plan-'

'Huh? Health and safety? I thought it was just a school gig.' It was more a grunt than a laugh, but as she glanced at his face she saw he'd relaxed a little. Ice broken. 'Or are you planning to do something very dangerous to me?'

Planning, no? Thinking, possibly. Fantasising, definitely. Just being in the same air as him was dangerous enough.

As he sat next to her on the couch his leg brushed against hers. Pursing her lips together, she clamped down on the fizz of electricity shooting through her.

This was unreal. The room was alive with vibrations of their moods. So many things remained unsaid, unresolved;

everything was amplified and tangible, mirrored in her erratic heartbeat and the sheen of sweat forming on her brow.

At his proximity she shifted slightly but was thwarted by the thick deep cushions that hemmed her in. His face was too close. He was too close. And just thinking that, breathing him in, sent whispers of something she hadn't felt in a very long time. A low-down tingling, parts of her body aching for his touch.

Well, heck, she couldn't be attracted to him, not in a real sense. From a distance, sure—who wouldn't be turned on by the idea of him? By his sex-god rock-star image? But those kinds of feelings were wishful thinking and daydreams. Not hard reality. Not gut-churning, tachycardia-inducing, libido-stirring reality.

Crazy feelings whirled in her chest, chaotic. Vivid. Hot. Very, very hot. 'It's…er…regulatory…you know.'

He grinned. 'What is? Doing dangerous things to rock stars? I like the sound of that—what do you have in mind?'

Well, she certainly wouldn't be telling him that. 'Obviously the school board needs a safety plan, the choir needs an action plan…'

'Aha…'

'But basically I just turn up to the school hall on the arranged night, do my stuff then leave? It's hardly rocket science. I'll do an unplugged set, so we won't need my band. And if the kids could learn a couple of my songs then we could all sing together in an encore. That's how it usually goes.'

Nate shoved his hands in his pockets and inhaled, inadvertently breathing in the smell of…yeah, sunshine. Stupid as it sounded. Like a lame lyric destined for the trash, but it was true—there was something fresh and new and bright about her.

'Sure, we've been working on a few of your hits already.

They love your stuff.' Her nose wrinkled as she gave him a brief smile. 'Maybe you could stay for a little while after and do some autographs…at least for the choir members.'

'I'm not planning on hanging round and having a big happy reunion with anyone. I don't see the point in nostalgia, do you?'

She blinked, a slight catch in her throat as she spoke, 'No. No, not at all. The past is best left alone. Agreed?'

'Couldn't have said it better myself.' Repetition made reality. *The past is best left alone.* Including ex-girlfriends who had started to haunt his dreams.

In truth he should have got Dario to sort this, as usual; Nate was far too busy to deal with schedules. So call it self-indulgent or just plain dumb, but the thought of seeing her before he went back to LA appealed. More than he wanted to admit.

She was his connection to his past, the experiences that had shaped him, given him the verve to fight hard for what he wanted.

A vibe hovered between them. He'd had lots of vibes before with lots of women. But this was bigger, stronger than ever. He ignored it. Tried to ignore it.

But he couldn't help looking at her, mesmerised by how the simple halter-neck dress with the daisy pattern and flared skirt, the same blue as her eyes, accentuated her fine collarbones. How her hair looked pull-down ready, and how his hand itched to reach out and let the curls flow over her shoulders.

She was gorgeous. Not Cara gorgeous, but then he'd spent a lot of time trying to work out which parts of her were real and which were fake. Certainly, her outspoken ministrations of everlasting love had been false. Everlasting. Pah. In Hollywood everlasting meant five minutes. But then, Sasha had promised him a lifetime too, and look where that had ended.

Man, this was wild. He forced out a breath. He'd forgotten all about her, consigned her to bad history and pushed her to the dark recesses of his brain. Now here she was invading every thought, his space, the flame of red hair looking pretty darned perfect against the cream couch.

But self-indulgence had been too costly in the past and he'd do well to remember that. Sasha might have held his heart once, but she'd damned near thrashed it too. Taking her to bed would be mighty fine, but he'd never trust her with anything more. Never again.

Staring at the papers in her hand, she shrugged. 'We're planning on doing the concert in two weeks' time. Saturday. The twenty-eighth. Spring Bank Holiday weekend.'

'Two weeks? You don't mess about.'

'I told you we were running out of time.'

And there went his month's holiday in Italy. 'I'll get Dario to handle the details, make sure I'm in town.'

'That would be great. Brilliant.' But she didn't look pleased.

'So, what's the problem now?' Crazy, but without thinking he touched her cheek. She curled into his touch briefly, before shifting out of reach, the papers hovering in her hand in mid-air. Her gaze dropped to her lap, but he didn't miss the flash of fire in her eyes and that stoked something in him too. 'You don't seriously want me to be interested in the details?'

'Why wouldn't you be? It's your show. And it makes things run smoothly if we're all on the same page.'

He looked at the papers in neat pink plastic folders all with little stickies on them. 'Which page exactly? You have so many.'

'There's nothing wrong with planning, Nate.'

'Sure. But that's what I pay someone else to do. I see you're still a walking-talking stationery cupboard. You haven't got a smartphone app for all this?'

'I prefer hard copy. It's easier if you can see it all laid out.'

'It's easier if I don't see it at all.' Planning in minutiae had always been Sasha's way of coping after her father's death—of ensuring the ordered life and stability she'd wanted. He used to think her organisational OCD was quirky and endearing, the way she'd carry her diary around religiously and check things, plan. If it hadn't been for her management skills he wouldn't have secured the gigs and the subsequent recording contract.

Their whole future had been mapped out at one point, down to the number of kids they were going to have, and when. He'd had a lucky break there, he'd always thought, when it was over.

Whereas Cassie—she'd always been happy-go-lucky, life's too short sort. Far too scatty for his liking. And serious Suzy, the eldest, had just put her head down and worked hard to protect them all. Three girls hit in different ways by one tragedy.

Then it occurred to him that the gents'-toilet fiasco would have pretty much killed Sasha. Her plans gone awry, then finding herself in his car. All out of her control. She liked to play safe.

And he didn't.

She looked so enthusiastic about her files he decided to indulge her. What did a few more minutes matter? 'Okay, sweet thing, hit me with it. And if I nod off, then, literally, hit me with it.'

An eyebrow peaked. 'Aww, your poor addled rock-star brain can't handle a few simple facts and figures?'

'Hey, I can handle anything you throw at me. Numbers, forecasts, projections. Do your worst.' He stretched his arms out and clicked his fingers. 'Bring it on.'

'You know your problem? You're all talk.'

'What, and no action? That's a dangerous gauntlet you're

throwing at me. You'd want to be very careful.' He held her gaze, wondering what she'd do if he just leaned in and covered that mouth with his. Would she drop the brisk schoolteacher act? Would she kiss him back?

The vibe tugged and tightened.

'Just an observation.' She swallowed. 'And, according to Cassie, careful is my middle name. Now listen.' Laughing nervously, she kicked off her shoes, shuffled up against the arm of the couch and faced him, fingertips running over the lines of ink. Making a good pretence that the heat in the room hadn't just hit scorching point. 'We have to cover the cost of train fares, hotels, my supply-teacher salary for a couple of days…I've broken it down into individual child cost, just for ease, so each one has a personal target to aim for…'

All he could see was page after page of graphs and squiggly lines. Her voice rose and fell in her schoolteacher voice as, head dipped, she focused on every darned detail.

But it gave him a chance to watch her, the tight swallow at her throat as she spoke, the tap of her toes. His gaze tiptoed up her legs, to the folds in her skirt, the tight cinch of her waist. He remembered how his hands had fitted around that waist ten years ago. Looked as if that couldn't happen now—but he liked her filled out a little.

His foolish heart tripped as his eyes travelled up the swell of her breast to her neck, the curve of her lips. And he realised she was frowning.

'Nathan? I said, are we done?'

Before he could stop himself he reached out and tilted her chin so he could see her eyes again. The heat there lit a fire in his gut and he was hit with a sudden need to know if her lips tasted just the way he remembered. 'Hell, Sasha, I don't know. Are we?'

CHAPTER FOUR

So this is where you leave.

Sasha stared up into those honeyed eyes, hazy now with only one thing. One unmistakable thing: desire. A shiver of excitement, and fear, tripped down her spine as heat pooled low in her abdomen. An energy buzzed around them, dancing and jumping with every second he held his fingers against her skin. Suddenly, leaving wasn't as easy as it sounded.

He wasn't supposed to want her. And she sure as heck wasn't supposed to want him back. This was a working relationship. Strictly platonic. Strictly professional.

Strictly temporary.

Edging away from his hands, she fixed a smile she hoped was distinctly non-sensual. Even though she sure as heck felt the most sensual she'd felt in aeons. 'I think that's all I needed to tell you. Questions?'

'None. As always, you're very thorough. Very…impressive.' Judging where his eyes were scrutinising now, she got the feeling Nathan wasn't talking about the reams of paper in her hands or the hours she'd spent on the spreadsheets.

And if he just leaned in a few more inches…

If she leaned forward…

Oh, hell. Seriously? She wanted to kiss him? She fought for a breath.

Maybe it was the champagne lulling her into a false

sense of…*in*security? Because there was nothing secure about the way her heart hammered or her legs weakened. Or the way he was looking at her with possession written all over his beautiful face.

She tore her eyes from his gaze, but they flatly refused to leave his face. Instead, she drank in the thick dark lashes, sculpted cheekbones and strong stubbled jaw. Everything about him screamed confidence, strength, sex appeal.

But more than that, he'd agreed to help her, at a huge personal cost. He'd given her time to go through the details when she knew she probably didn't give a damn, indulging her for no one's benefit but her own.

That just about blew off the assumptions that he was a selfish sex-crazed raiser. Who knew there was a softer side too? Strident. Complicated, not one dimensional like his media persona.

For goodness' sake, where did he get off being kind? And where did that leave her?

Captivated? Hot. Yes, too hot. And aching to feel the press of his mouth on hers.

When she spoke her voice was shaky. 'Why did you invite me over when we could have talked all this through on the phone?'

'Direct as ever. I wanted to see you.' The spark in his eyes swirled with confusion now.

'And what Nate Munro wants, Nate Munro gets, right?'

'Usually.' He shrugged. 'I just had a…feeling about you. Your last entrance made quite an impression. I wondered what you could possibly do for an encore, but I wasn't expecting spreadsheets. Women usually employ other techniques to get me to do things with them.' He laughed. 'You're definitely one of a kind.'

That was new—no one ever had feelings about her. She tried hard to be unobtrusive and not draw attention to herself. Fighting the heat whooshing through her now, making her unsteady and unsure, she swallowed deeply through a dry throat. 'A feeling?'

'Yes, I don't know. A hunch.' But he clearly didn't want to elaborate. For a man famous for heavy, heart-on-your-sleeve rock ballads that wooed the world's women, he kept way too much wrapped up inside when it mattered. 'Why did you agree to come if we could have just talked it through on the phone?'

'Cassie made me. Suzy, of course, would have a fit if she knew I was here.' And no way was she going to admit the guy had been burning a hole in her brain for twenty-four hours.

'Suzy. Suzy.' He shook his head, his mouth kicking up into a rueful half-smile. 'So forthright and ardent and so… righteous. How many times did she warn you off me?'

'Too many to count.' It had been a battle of wills in the end: the more Suzy told her no, the more Sasha had said yes. To Nate. 'But I never took any notice of her.'

'Until the end. Seems she was right after all.'

That he was wrong for her? That he was bad through and through? That he'd break Sasha's heart? 'Yes, I guess she was.'

Her big sister had been right about all of that. But Sasha had ignored the warnings. Just as she was ignoring the alarms blaring in her ears now.

Go. Walk away. She'd got what she wanted from him. Hadn't she? 'So. Is that it? I should go now.'

'Unless…' His hand was on her arm now.

'I don't…I can't…' Can't think.

'Hush, Sasha. I don't want anything you don't want to give.' He'd said that line before too. And she'd ached to give him everything, but every single time she'd stopped short. Unable to truly let go. With him, or anyone else since.

His voice was thick and gruff as the pad of his thumb stroked along her arm, and it felt as if he were stroking her insides too. Her breathing matched his as his fingers wound up the back of her neck, her nerve endings on full alert, rooting her to the spot. 'I'd forgotten just how beautiful you are. How intensely you feel things. Ten years, but you haven't changed so much.'

'You want to bet? If you think I'm still that little lost girl I used to be then you're very mistaken. I've worked hard to be who I am now. I've changed more than you could imagine.'

'Yes.' He smiled as he unhooked a strand of her hair that had caught in her dress strap, then he glanced down her body. 'I guess you have.'

Oh, God. She didn't want him touching her in some sort of rose-coloured grasp at something they'd had, too long ago. Rewinding wouldn't achieve anything but heartache, and moving forward meant grasping her self-respect and waiting for Mr Right, not grabbing a quickie on a couch— however nice—with Mr Very Wrong.

Typical, the first time in years her hormones were demanding usage, and it just had to happen with Mr So-Far-From-Safe not even one of her health and safety policies could help her.

Her hand reached to his hard wall of chest to push him away. But the feel of his T-shirt beneath her palm, and the heat of his skin beneath that, made her fingers curl into the fabric.

His face closed in, his eyes telling her what he wanted, his so familiar spicy scent weaving round her in a sensual web. Breathing became laboured as she waited for the moment she felt his lips against hers. Waiting to see if he still kissed the same way after all this time.

His head inclined towards her but he paused, his face swimming with a mixture of emotions, the most profound of which was confusion. Giving her just enough time for her doubts to jump in and fill the gap.

Wiggle away from the sex god, Sasha.

She knew who she was now, what she wanted, and it definitely wasn't inviting trouble back into her life.

Finding strength from who knew where, she pushed him gently away, then swung her feet to the floor and slipped on her shoes. 'I don't think *this* is a good idea, Nathan. It might be the way you crazy rock stars roll, but it's not how I do things.' Or was this how he wanted to be paid for his help?

Yikes.

'What? Have you invented a whole new way of *doing things* in Chesterton? In LA-LA land we usually start with a kiss and then see how things pan out…'

'Nothing's going to pan out. Is it just a game to you? Something for old times' sake? Play the silly ex-girlfriend and see how far you can get. What happened to leaving the past alone?'

'I was just getting caught up in the moment.' His smile was genuine and warm and reflected in his eyes. Which made her feel even worse. He stood calmly and offered her his hand. 'And so were you.'

Good point. 'But I can't just live in a moment, Nate. My life's not a wild ride like yours. I have responsibilities, I have to work, to pay the mortgage, I have to be a good role model to my students. Moments don't count, the big picture does.'

Her sister Cassie would kiss and walk away without a second's thought. No, Cassie would stay the night and not have a qualm. Cassie would relish the chance of grasping a little vicarious fame, enjoy the buzz of being with a celebrity.

But Sasha wasn't Cassie. She couldn't do the one-kiss thing, and definitely not the one-night thing. She was a forever girl, plain and simple, so there was no way she'd let herself get carried away with him. Especially not to then watch him leave again.

Shaking his touch away as quickly as she could, she smoothed down her dress and her nerves. 'I'll see you at the gig in two weeks. Thanks for taking the time to see me. And for helping in this project.'

'No, seriously, the pleasure was all mine.' But his eyes had darkened and he looked as bewildered as she felt. Standing up, he reached for the hotel phone. 'I'll call the car.'

'You'll do no such thing. I can find my way home from Mayfair.' The further she got away from him, the better. And quickly. Spending time in his car with his people wouldn't help her a jot. And she didn't need to owe him any more. The one lesson she'd learned from her father's suicide—never owe anyone anything.

Nate captured her gaze and shook his head in an *I'll-never-understand-you* kind of gesture, but eventually capitulated to her firm stance. 'Then at least let me walk you to the tube.'

'No. I'm just fine. Thank you. I can manage the tube—' And then she remembered their phone conversation, his chat with Dario the bear in the gent's.

Her hand covered her mouth in horror. She'd been about to commit the most heinous sin in her own book: kissing a man who was already committed to someone else. Her brain had clearly fried with lust. 'And what about your girlfriend?'

'Girlfriend? I haven't got—'

'The other night, after the gig, didn't you have a date? And then…eugh, the tramp twins in the limo? What kind of person are you, Nathan?'

'Misunderstood?' His hands curled into tight fists as bewilderment turned to bitterness. 'Story of my life.'

'I've pegged you as a lot of things over the years, reading reports of you drinking yourself into oblivion, partying for days on end, and hooking up with the most…' she tried to think of a word that didn't sound as condemning or derogatory as her thoughts '…quirky of girlfriends. But I never thought of you as someone who uses women. Not until now.'

Grabbing her handbag, she dashed to the door and down the stairs as quickly as she could.

Only when she'd reached the tube station did she realise that, along with her pride, she'd left her messenger bag and files on his couch. *Goddamn.* The man was turning her brain to a soggy hot mess.

But there was no way she was going back to fetch them, not tonight. Not when she'd had to rip her body away from him. Not when she had only one thing on her mind where Nate Munro was concerned. And it certainly didn't include a whole lot of paper.

Insane.

Yep. Insane in every aspect. Nate stood outside the grimy red brick walls of his old high school and felt the familiar tightening in his gut. How he'd allowed himself to be talked into this he didn't know. And by a woman who hadn't changed much at all no matter how much she protested to the contrary. She still shot first and asked questions…never.

Don't ask, but jump to conclusions. Check.

Don't give him a chance to explain. Check.

That was Sasha all over.

Just being here in this rundown dead-end school was bad enough, never mind spending more time with her.

He found her in the old school hall. Nothing had changed here either—the whole scenario was as if he'd rewound ten years to his adolescent nightmares. If this was the punishment for being the bad boy of rock, he was definitely going to work on his game from now on.

The place still smelt of sweaty socks and cheap lemon

air freshener. Still had scuffs in the dirty cream paintwork, and old velvet curtains that didn't quite fit the stage. Where she was standing. In front of a gaggle of kids who, as it happened, made quite a good noise.

'Sorry to interrupt…' He waited for her to turn round. Watched the silent gasp, the irritated raise of her eyebrows, the flush of her cheeks. The hesitant smile as she saw her bag in his hand.

Sunshine streamed through an upper window, casting bright light across the stage in a perfect arc, catching dust motes dancing almost in rhythm with the song.

Even from this distance he could see the different hues in her hair, not just red, but gold and blonde too, drifting down her back, shimmering with every move.

Goddamn she was sexy. And so different from the women he usually dated. First off, she'd said no to him. *Again*. That never happened.

She wasn't lured by his fame or his wealth; in fact far from that, she didn't want a dime of it for herself. Which was refreshing and curious. And the fact she'd left without taking advantage of what he'd had to offer pushed intriguing to the top of the list of adjectives he already had for her.

She wore another fifties' summery dress today, short capped sleeves, tight V neck and full skirt in a soft green that accentuated her waist and fell in feminine folds to her knees. Demure enough to be suitable for her job, it was cut from some kind of thin fabric that made you want to touch it. Touch her.

Holding her finger towards him to signal him to wait, she led the choir through a medley of three recent number one hits, none of them his, while they performed a quirky dance routine at the same time. A mix of above-average talent and ability, they had enough charisma to pull at the heartstrings of any benevolent audience, but probably not enough to win any prizes. Yet.

Sasha was good with them too. Praising and cajoling when the more timid ones forgot the words, or were reluctant to walk to the front of the stage. Singing along with them in her soft lyrical voice that swung him back to a time he'd be better off forgetting. Swaying her hips as she conducted. Her head tipping back with a gentle laugh as one of them played the fool, then bringing them back to focus again and finishing the song.

Dragging his eyes from her backside, he watched the choir fine-tune the dance moves. One kid in particular caught his eye. So similar to Marshall it made his heart constrict into a tight fist. With his eager wide eyes, too big tongue and dazzling smile he was, as far as Nate was concerned, the star of the show. Just as Marshall had been.

And suddenly the urge to escape across the hardwood floor threatened to overwhelm him. It was too much to relive all at once. Chesterton High. Marshall. Sasha. Too many dark memories he'd worked hard at pushing to the farthest corner of his mind in a blur of hard alcohol and commitment-free sex. Good sex, too. Fast, hot, hard. Sex that had taught him how to be a man, how to please a woman.

Not the kind of sex Sasha would want, all fluff and fairy tales and diarised on her planner. Every Wednesday and Saturday, missionary position only.

He dumped her bag on a chair and turned to leave, but at that moment the choir stopped singing and he heard her voice. 'Guys, I have a visitor I need to talk to. Go through your steps again, from the top. George, you count them in. I won't be long.'

Good, neither would he. 'Security here sucks. I walked straight in and no one batted an eyelid.'

'Nate, it's a school. Public property, really. People come and go all day. Besides, it's four o'clock and almost everyone's gone home. You hardly look like a potential threat.

Hmm…much.' She looked at the baseball cap pulled down over his face and the dark sunglasses disguising his features. Then her gaze stole a quick glance down his black leather jacket and dark jeans.

Her eyes fired with something akin to want. After ten years in this job he knew when a woman wanted him. After two years of loving her he knew when Sasha wanted him too.

Which was all kinds of a turn-on.

'You're risking a mobbing, though. I don't think the kids have worked out they're sharing the same air as Nate Munro, but once they do you'll be swamped.'

'I can handle it.' He nodded to the hall door where Dario stood watch. 'And I have back-up.'

'Oh, Tweedle Dum. How nice.' She waved her fingers over to his manager-cum-minder, who, true to form, did not move a muscle. 'Are you two joined at the hip? That must make your love life very interesting.'

'Aww, he's very discreet. And he's not the jealous type.'

Her eyebrows peaked. 'Really? Could have fooled me.'

'Well, maybe just a little bit, but he has my best interests at heart.'

'He has a heart? Funny.' Stacking chairs along the side wall, she shrugged. 'And clearly I'm not on his list of Nate interests.'

'He thinks this whole project is too distracting.' That was the polite way of describing Dario's reaction. At her frown he smiled and went to help dismantle the rest of the rows of plastic seats. He just couldn't help but wind her up, watch the pink tinge her cheeks. 'And, for the record, my sex life can be very interesting. As interesting as you like, Sasha.'

'Whoa. Down boy. Er…girlfriend?'

'Will you ever listen? There is no girlfriend.' And that was all she needed to know. Private time needed to remain so. There was sex, which he did, and there was dating, which he didn't. 'Is your opinion so low of me that you think I'd do something as crass as run with two women at the same time?'

'Wasn't there a leery story once about you and blonde triplets? Really, and I always thought three was a crowd.'

He smiled at the memory. That had been fun, even though the journalist had exaggerated the details beyond any semblance of truth. But recently he'd lost his appetite for hard and fast with adoring strangers.

'Don't believe everything you read. I might be bad but I do have some morals. Like helping hapless choir teachers when I could be doing something infinitely more relaxing. Here, I brought this.'

He offered her the bag containing way too much paper. No matter how much he'd wanted to scroll through it to find clues about her life he'd managed to keep his eyes away. Her business was her business.

And *her* private life? Yep, damn right he wanted to know more about that. Far more than was good for him.

As she took the bag her line of vision tracked back to the kids on stage. She shifted position, inadvertently stepping a little closer, flowers and vanilla and something… something that made his heart beat a little faster enveloping him. 'What do you think?'

'I think…' She really did not need to know what thoughts were running round his head. 'I'll see you at the concert.' Dario was right: she was distracting. Flirting was all well and good, but with his body reacting so strongly to her the best thing he could do was get out. Fast.

'Oh. Don't you like the choir? I realise we could do with some help.'

Yes, they could. But it was not going to come from him. 'Well, yes, but I have to go.'

'Could you at least tell me your first impressions? Some

pointers?' Her shoulders twitched backwards and the beginning of a pout hovered over her lips.

He huffed out a breath. Seemed she wasn't going to let him off lightly. She held him there with her teacher stare that simultaneously scared the pants off him and turned him on.

'Okay. I like the mash-up, it's a clever mix. But you need to focus more on the harmony in the second verse of "Sunshine Smile", it gets lost, and that whole riff needs simplifying…' He paused to watch her bemused reaction.

'Oh…really? Are you sure?'

'You did ask. If it doesn't suit, then don't change a thing. But you'll be sorry you didn't.' He fought the urge to bury his face in that vibrant hair and tried to refocus on the choir. Not easy. 'While you're at it you should drop the tenors just for that verse, see if it sounds less…busy. And the alto needs to be stronger in "Ways of a Saint"…have you thought about a more abrupt ending instead of the way it finishes on the original?'

'Whoa…slow down.' She held her palms up, scrabbled round for a pen and paper and started jotting down bullet points. 'Isn't that a bit radical?'

'No. You've got to give them something that surprises them. Trust me. This is my job, I live and breathe this kind of stuff.' He hadn't even started, but pointing out all their failings would take time he didn't have. And he didn't much like the idea of hanging around this hall, with all its ghosts and memories, for the next millennia.

'Do you want to walk the kids through your ideas? I'm sure it'd be better coming from you.'

'What? Me? Teach? Them? No, thanks. Like I said, I've got to go.' Always the outsider, he'd never felt as if he'd belonged in this place so there were no warm fuzzies or sentimental reasons keeping him here. None at all. Nothing to compel him to help any more than he already had.

'What? Mr Fabulous and oh-so wild, Mr Off His Head Crazy…scared of a bunch of mixed-ability kids?' She laughed. 'That's hysterical.'

He couldn't see a funny side. 'I'm just busy. Not scared.'

'Prove it, hot-shot music man. Prove you're not scared.' The paper fluttered to the floor as she stared him down, her eyes a mix of serious intent and a playful tease that tugged at long-buried heartstrings.

Prove it. Her mouth formed the words but no sound accompanied them. For a moment he thought she might stick out her tongue as well.

'Don't be immature.'

Then her voice came, soft and appealing. 'Imagine how fantastic it would have been if you'd had a mentor all those years ago. If someone had helped you, even for a few minutes. It might have made such a difference. What have you got to lose?'

She was right. Guidance was scant back then. No one was interested in a loud-mouthed kid with an over-inflated sense of musical skill and entitlement. But…if someone had helped…

He shook his head, shocked he was even considering this…but even if he didn't make a difference to their performance, getting involved could surely make some amends to the damage he'd wreaked when he was young and stupid. When he'd thought he knew what was best, and that the only way to solve problems involved a whole lot of aggression riding on a surge of testosterone.

These kids needed help.

Looking at their hopeful faces, he suddenly didn't want to be the one to poop on their parade. And if that meant he spent more time with Sasha, then so be it. He could keep a lid on his libido.

'Okay. I can spare a few minutes. Bring that boy…' he

pointed to the Marshall lookalike, saw the big open grin and the thick palms, the intense need to please '…and…'

And just like that his past came crowding back in on him along with a host of emotions he didn't want. His voice caught as a dull ache gripped his chest. 'Yes…more to the front, he's got great rhythm and clearly loves it. You need enthusiasm like that to carry such a happy song.'

Sasha glanced at the boy and then back at Nate. And clearly he hadn't been hiding his feelings too well, because tears filled her eyes and she pressed a palm to her chest. 'Oh, Nate. I'm so sorry.'

That was all he needed, her pity.

Back off. Because, in truth, Sasha was the only person in the world who'd understand the pain of losing Marshall. That was a part of his life he never shared and he wasn't re-visiting any of it again in a hurry. Not when she was within reach-out-and-hold distance.

'Yeah, me too.' Forcing his voice through the Rock of Gibraltar that had lodged in his throat, he focused back on the kids. The ones that mattered now, the ones he could help. 'Right, let's get this act whipped into shape, shall we?'

CHAPTER FIVE

'Miss Sweet, is that…is that Nate Munro?'

Readjusting back to the choir took monumental effort. Sasha had been too busy watching the colour in Nate's cheeks bleed away at the memory of Marshall. And she realised at that moment how difficult it must have been for him to come back here. How much she was in his debt that he'd even stepped foot in this hall.

Nate had protected his brother, had fought for him to attend mainstream school at a time when Down's syndrome kids were often regarded as unteachable. And he'd taught them all to embrace differences. So losing his beloved Marshall so young must have been devastating.

She of all people knew how hard it was to lose someone you poured your love into. How difficult to restart your life. How much you clung to a safety raft, the familiar, the known. Because the unknown was too terrible to contemplate. And how you avoided reaching for those painful memories at all cost.

And yet here he was. Making her challenge her assumptions of the kind of man he was.

But now the barriers were up again.

She caught his eye, unsure of how to answer George's question. Of course the kids would click they were in the company of someone important. Just one look at him and his star quality shone through. The dark edgy clothing, his diffident stance that was accentuated with every confident footstep. The whisky-deep voice.

Whispering across the hall, she tried to coax him forward. 'Well? What do you want me to say? I wouldn't try lying—they're not daft.'

'Busted.' Removing his baseball cap, glasses and hoodie, he walked to the edge of the stage and looked up into their wide-eyed faces, smiled at the collective sharp intake of breath. 'Hi. Yes, pleased to meet you all. I'm Nate.'

Her own intake of breath was as instinctive as the choir's. But for a whole different reason. She hoped. Sure, they were blown away by his elevated celebrity status, the face that peered out from magazine racks on the high street. But she just couldn't get used to—or tire of—the way his body moved so fluidly, the way his jeans hugged his toned thighs and appeared not to want to let go.

The taut breadth of his chest, black collared shirt open enough—no, never enough—for her to glimpse the gift of his body underneath. That Californian sunshine sure had kissed his body. And, for a split second, Sasha wondered just how far down that tan went.

'Ahem…it's *Mr* Munro to you lot.' She grinned, finding her breath again and trying to talk over the squeals of excitement. 'We have manners, remember, No Limits choir. Mr Munro has agreed to help us with our fundraising concert, but we have to keep his visit here quiet. He's a busy man and he doesn't need the hassle of a zillion screeching fans every time he comes here—we can save that for concert night. And we have to show him we can be professional too, and listen. And do what we are told. Give me two more minutes while I chat to our guest.'

'Scary teacher voice,' Nathan muttered under his breath and leaned closer, the fresh heat in his eyes melting the sadness she'd seen moments before. And sending a flush to her cheeks, direct hit.

'You haven't seen anything yet,' she whispered back to him out of the corner of her mouth. 'They don't call me Miss Sweet and Sour for nothing.'

'Sweet and Sour? Ouch.' One eyebrow raised as he met her wry smile with one of his own. 'That sucks.'

'It's original, I guess, and they obviously think enough of me to make up a nickname. I try not to be too hard on them. It's a tough area and life's difficult enough as it is. I'm more about building them up than shooting them down.'

'I wish we'd had more teachers like you at school. Ones that gave a damn.' The sentence was loaded with memories, but he smiled back at her, the energy in the air smoothing into something less fraught.

She wondered whether she'd imagined the intense heat in his eyes. But as she risked another glance there was still a warm spark there, simmering, that set her pulse jittering. 'Some days I could cheerfully scream. They have a habit of knowing which buttons to push.'

'But you obviously love it regardless, Miss Sweet and Sour.'

'I get a kick out of helping people, realising potential. It's all I ever wanted to do.' Harnessing her energy into something positive instead of dwelling on the negatives of her life.

'I remember. You wanted to be a music teacher just like Mr Taylor. You had a crush on him.'

'I did not.' She laughed, remembering the very bohemian long-haired music teacher who'd opened up a new world to her. Sure, Mr Taylor had inspired her, but the only person she'd had a crush on in her school years was Nathan Munro.

'You followed him around for the whole of fourth form like a lost puppy.' He leaned close to her ear. 'That's when I started to get jealous.'

If she edged just a little closer they'd be touching. Hip to hip.

Trouble was, she didn't want simple touching, not where he was concerned. She wanted what every hot-blooded woman would want faced with him in close proximity. And that frightened her.

To stop making a fool of herself in front of the whole choir and Mr Celebrity here she shook free and busied herself with the long-lost contents of her bag.

'You weren't even going out with me then.'

'No, but you were very definitely on my radar.'

And he'd been on hers. Out of her league, the cool loner who never quite seemed to belong to one gang or other and had dangerous written all over him. Some things hadn't changed. He still had the remarkable ability to set her on edge. And, worse, after ten years of putting him well behind her, she was reacting like a giddy teenager all over again.

She kept her voice steady and attempted to regain some composure. 'Okay, let's get this thing going. And you, Mr Obnoxious, stand right over there. Away.' *From me.* She ushered him to the back of the hall. 'It's better acoustics.'

An hour and a stratospheric improvement in the choir later Dario tapped Nate on the shoulder. 'Time to go to your next appointment, Nate.'

'Oh, yeah? What is it this time?' Thank God he had someone with their eye on the ball, because right now he was way too engrossed to think of what next.

'De Facto Art Space on Portobello.'

'Okay. Five minutes.' Nate sighed inwardly. And he was having such a good time, a surprisingly good time.

Not least the fact the choir had listened and performed far better than he could have imagined, but working with Sasha had proved easy and fun. She was a natural with the kids and brought out the best in them. Her refreshing honesty and openness made him believe there were some genuine people left in the world. Maybe not in his world. But out here, in reality, away from his chaos.

'I'll be outside waiting. Is she coming too?' Dario nodded towards Sasha as she packed her bag and waved the last stragglers off home.

Another insane idea.

She grimaced at them both, eyes wide. '*She*? Who? Me?' She touched her chest. 'Thank you for such a kind and genuine invitation, but I wouldn't want to cramp the Tweedle twins' style. Besides I have an assembly to prepare…then, paint to watch dry.'

But when her lips curved into such a sweet smile and her eyes shone with teasing Nate didn't want this afternoon to end so quickly. He only had a few hours with her all up— maybe one more rehearsal, then the actual show. Then he'd be out of her life, out of this jaunt into a past he'd stuffed at the back of his mind. A few more hours wouldn't hurt. No big deal. His schedule meant he'd be gone soon enough.

And then what?

More sleepless nights wondering, what if? His imagination running wild over what she wore under those demure dresses, how her bare skin would feel against his, how her cute mouth would taste.

Just once.

He rubbed a hand across the back of his neck. What was he doing? Inviting her to ruin his life again? He knew what being with her cost. How much she'd trampled over everything they'd had. Thrown their relationship back in his face. And yet…he couldn't seem to help himself.

It was a shock, that was all. Meeting her again after so long, wanting to learn more about her, to see how much she'd changed. Finding answers to those half-asked questions that had flitted through his brain every now and then. People reconnected all the time these days—social media was awash with reunited friends.

Normal. Natural. Nothing to get hung up about.

'So you'd really rather stay home than come to a party of celebrities drinking carb-free wine and eating organic macro-vegan canapés? I just don't understand you, sweet thing.'

'Wow.' She laughed. 'You A-listers certainly know how to have a good time. Shame I'm so busy.' She curled a lock of hair round her finger and looked up at him through her fringe. 'Did I mention I was going to cook old-fashioned bangers and mash, with lashings of butter, and onion gravy?'

'Temptress.' He stepped forward and his arm brushed against hers. Like a kid on a first date at the movies, breathless and overflowing with testosterone, he felt the shock and static as they touched. And was it his imagination or did she jump too?

'No, not at all.' She shrugged away and flashed a non-chalant grin. 'It's been a long day. I'm just hungry.'

'Me too. Starving.' Just not for food.

But duty pulled at him. 'The artist's a good friend of mine. I promised I'd go. If the trendy food doesn't tempt you, maybe the art will? It's Rocco Baldini.'

'Rocco?' Her eyes grew large. 'Really? Ohmygod, you know him? Some of his work is…well, amazing.'

Excellent. He'd got her on the hook. Now he just had to reel her in. 'I know. I have one of his installations at my house in Malibu. I'll introduce you if you like.'

'Ooh, gosh, no. I wouldn't know what to say.' Strapping her bag over her shoulder, she walked to the door and flicked off the hall lights. The corridor was empty and shadowed. 'Since when were you into art?'

'There's so much about me you don't know.'

'Oh? I thought since you were such a big media star we all knew everything about you. You certainly live your life out on the page, on the stage…'

'Don't be so naive. I collect art and good wine…race motorbikes, own a gym… You want a copy of my resumé?' He took her arm and walked her through the school, fighting the urge to push her up against the lockers as he used to way back when. 'How about you spend a few more hours with me finding out what I'm really like? Put some of your assumptions to the test? No strings.'

'I can't. I told you—'

'Can't? Or won't? Or…scared? Scared that you might be wrong about me?' He drew to a halt outside room B4. Music class. Where he'd first found the courage to ask her out on a date.

This was a stupid place to come and bring back a host of memories. He had to get out. His hand was on her arm and he searched her eyes for some kind of agreement. Something that said he wasn't the only crazy one here.

But all he found was amusement, shock and a frown that said he was on dangerous ground. 'No. I'm not scared.'

'So…prove it.' He made a pretty poor attempt at her teacher scowl.

She shook her head and laughed. 'Oh, God. How did I not see that coming?'

'Two can play at that game, Miss Sweet and Sour. Besides, one good turn deserves another, right? I need a little help here. I hate going to this kind of place alone, where I'll have to waffle on about texture and depth and stuff.'

'Is that because you wouldn't know what it was? Depth?'

'Hey, I can do deep.'

'Sure. Nothing says deep like a quickie with two hot blondes with big bazookas, followed by a date with a whole different woman.'

'I didn't do that.'

'You were going to.'

'Can't blame a guy for trying.' Seriously, she had no idea. 'That was just guy talk. I didn't do it. And I didn't have a date—it was just an excuse to get Dario off my back. Come on. You owe me. Big time.'

For the first time that afternoon her face grew serious, her eyes dark and hollow. She thought for a second, seemed to reconcile his words. 'I guess I do. Okay, you're right. You've been great with the kids and you're doing the concert—'

'So you'll come, save me from a night of pretentious boredom?'

'Just to help you out. Then the debt's repaid?' She looked down at her soft green dress and wedge sandals. 'I'll need to go home and change.'

'No, don't. I like the way you look, this whole vintage gig.'

'This whole *cheap* gig. Ferret around in junk shops often enough and you can find a real bargain. I like it though. It reminds me of an era when people were honest and faithful and…predictable. When life was safe.'

'Ah, yes.' He loved to watch her face as he teased her, see the dawning realisation. 'The nineteen fifties, time of the Cold War, the Iron Curtain, the threat of nuclear bombs… yes, very safe.'

'Okay.' Her whole face lit up as she smiled. 'So maybe I just like the clothes. They're pretty and feminine.'

'And as luck would have it, I happen to have a thing for big skirts.' Although it was more that he wanted to know what was going on under hers.

She rolled her eyes. 'But I don't think it'll work for tonight.'

'It works for me. It makes you stand out from the crowd, your own style. Unique.' Definitely unique. And if he gave her an out to go home she might change her mind again. He wasn't prepared to take that risk. 'You look amazing. Seriously, amazing. You'll give them all a run for their money.'

* * *

But Sasha didn't feel amazing. Not when she stepped out of the car to the flash of a thousand light bulbs. Not when all she could hear was the screech of Nate's name to look right, left, *who's the date? Who are you wearing?*

Who? Idiots. *Clothes,* she wanted to shout back. Can't you see? And they'd all die if they knew she'd bought hers from a Chesterton High Street charity shop.

'Scaato and Paul, Frederike,' Nate called back, in a language she didn't understand.

And she definitely didn't feel amazing when he leaned in and said, 'It's a bit of a maul but we just have to get through this bit.'

She didn't want to just get through. She wanted it to end. Didn't want them to see her, to ask who she was. She didn't want them to know. The last thing she needed was her past dragged through the papers all over again.

Plan A: she would stay long enough to be polite, then leave through the back door. Plan B? She'd come up with something…just as soon as he removed his distracting hand from her back.

He steered her into the sparse concrete-grey space. Once the front door closed behind them her heart rate normalised. Not many guests so far, but enough to keep the ambient noise above a whisper. And no more photographers.

What groups of people there were she recognised from the TV as they air kissed and *mwah-ed* their way round.

'I feel seriously underdressed,' she whispered.

'You look fine. You look—'

Nate brushed a curl back from her face and looked down at her, his dark eyes locked with hers. A ripple of heat engulfed her, sucking air out of her lungs, stalling her breath. Everything around her lost sharp focus, then he abruptly dropped his hand, startled by something—some war inside him that played out in the shadows of his cheeks. There was a flicker of doubt in those heated pupils, a question that he seemed to be pondering.

Like her. What was she doing here?

Flustered by his proximity, she dragged her eyes away from his, and refocused on the surroundings, trying to make the best of it. After all, it wasn't every day she was invited to such a schooshed-up event. 'This place is astonishing. I've never seen anything like it. Although, I guess for you it's nothing unusual. It's part of your job. A way of life.'

He shrugged. 'It *is* my life. Heart and soul.'

'You never think of stopping? Settling down? Family even?'

Oh, Lordy, where did that come from? She hoped her question didn't sound too much more than idle curiosity. Which it wasn't. Seriously. 'I read that you got engaged once.'

Again with the shrug. She got the feeling he'd brought the shutters down just a little the moment he'd felt her prying, or was it just before that? 'In this job if you stop, you die. Or your profile does, which is about the same thing. Truth is, I'm just not the settling kind.'

And she'd known it, so why her stomach contracted, just a little, she couldn't say. 'Do you get proper time off, ever?'

'No.'

Casting her eye around at all the beautiful people, she asked him, 'Do you have real friends?'

'As opposed to what? Imaginary ones? Because I grew out of those years ago. Of course I have friends.' In a swift motion he stepped back and spread his arms out. Laughed. 'I'm just a regular guy.'

A smile tugged at her mouth, just watching him laugh had a relaxing effect on her. 'Believe me, Nathan, there's nothing regular about you. Or this…'

She pulled her shoulders back and wandered through the cavernous room towards the bar refusing to be intimidated by the designer suits and sky-high heels, people who wouldn't know where Chesterton was or how desperately needy the area was. Who had never met a special-needs kid let alone fought for their rights.

And they were the poorer for it.

Unless, of course, she was being overly judgemental.

And spending time with Nate had shown her that she could be. She'd been wrong about him, after all. Was that how she'd become? Placing people in boxes, with labels? Was that what being safe meant? That she couldn't see further than her own experiences?

She rolled her neck from side to side, eased the muscles, and tried to relax.

Nate leaned against the bar with languorous ease, his legs crossed at the ankles, sleeves rolled up. A regular guy at a regular work function. Worth about a trillion dollars. 'You want a drink, Sash? It might help you relax a little.'

'Just a fruit juice, please.' He had a way of making her want to do things she shouldn't, like attend pretentious parties, lean into his palm on the small of her back. Kiss him.

The thought buzzed round her head like an irritating wasp she couldn't waft away.

Kiss him!

Goodness, no.

So she'd be avoiding alcohol, because that would only lead her further into temptation.

'Let me see,' he said, with a mischievous glint in his eye. 'Fruit juice…lychee or durian?'

'What?' *Oh, merry hell. Beam me up.*

'Kidding.' As he laughed his leg brushed against hers causing a riot of tingling throughout her body. She didn't know if he even realised he was doing it. But by God, she wanted him to stop.

And to never stop.

'Okay, so no to the exotic fruit. How about…oranges that

have been pressed through the thighs of nubile virgins?' He handed her a glass of something thick and bright. 'That's very on trend at the moment.'

'No, darling, that was so last year.' She laughed and took the proffered drink. 'I'm glad you can see how strange this all seems to someone like me.'

'I suppose I've got used to it all. It is what it is.' He paused, his brow creased as he surveyed the room. 'I've never really thought about it, until now. I fell headlong into a life of crazy and it's just a part of me now.' He laughed. 'Some people go to any event to get themselves noticed. I'm more selective these days.'

Sasha shuddered. 'I don't understand this need to be seen. I'd hate having to face those cameras every day.' But then, perhaps not everyone had a past they wanted to keep out of the spotlight.

She followed him to the stark back walls, where bright orange oddly molded objects, made from what looked like balls of Plasticine, hung on tight steel chains.

People around them talked about light and structure and the profound meaning of such stark urban symbolism. Or something.

Nathan's eyebrows peaked and a little frown line appeared on his forehead. She fought an urge to trace her finger along it, down his cheek, to that mouth.

He whispered into her ear, his breath warming her skin. 'Do you like the art?'

She shook her head and bit her lip trying not to be thrown by a situation so utterly out of her comfort zone. Or by her body's irritating response to his every touch. 'Would it be rude if I said no?'

'It's worth a bomb.' His head tipped back as he focused longer on the piece. A laugh rose from his chest, full and hearty. 'But it looks like…earwax?'

'Yup. Thank goodness I'm not the only one to think

so.' As she laughed their gazes snagged again. One second. Two. Something snapped between them, electric and intense. Something deep. Something new. For a moment bewilderment flitted across his face.

'Better not tell Rocco what you think—he's coming over. Don't break his heart.'

A tall scruffy-looking man in an ill-fitting mismatched jacket and trousers sauntered over. He gave Nate a thump on the arm. 'Long time no see, mate. How ya dooin?'

'Great. This is my friend, Sasha.'

'Y'all reet?' The guy was called Rocco, but was from deepest Newcastle? She'd never heard him speak, famous as he was for his Silent Night series—living art that involved a bed, a mouth gag and handcuffs. Whacky didn't cut it.

She watched as Nathan engaged Rocco in quiet intense conversation. Where was the hell-raiser now? Talking knowledgeably about earwax installations and art spaces, drinking champagne and laughing. The more she discovered about him, the more she wanted to know. Which was all kinds of irritating.

He stepped forward as he spoke, and immediately a cold chill snaked up her back.

Ah. Clearly her body was just on physical overdrive. Lust. Hot and sharp, and not lasting.

Physical she could deal with. She had total control over her body; she could wrestle it into submission. It was the psychological she had trouble with. The knowledge that love was fragile, that had been reinforced with every going-nowhere relationship she'd had.

But to make things easy on herself she was going to activate Plan A. Just as soon as she could get a word in.

Edging back from the group, she leaned against the bar and took a moment to watch him in action.

Presently, a statuesque blonde glided by in a curve-hugging dress slashed up the sides and held together by transparent plastic panels. She gave Sasha a quick disappointed once-over, then linked her arm into Nate's and curled into his body like a cat eager for a stroke.

A cat on heat. Her manicured hand strayed to Nate's spectacular backside and squeezed possessively. Another of Nathan's conquests, clearly. Sasha presumed the room was full of them.

But even from here he looked surprised, embarrassed, although no one would ever have known it. His gaze hardened and his jaw twitched enough for Sasha to remember how similarly he'd reacted when he'd tried to cover up for his shortcomings as a youth.

'Jasmine. This is Sasha.' He steered the lofty blonde over. 'She's a friend of mine, from school.'

'Going back to your roots? How very retro of you. Clever boy,' the woman purred. 'Hi…er…Sara? Didn't have time to change? Never mind, you look adorable just as you are. Really.'

Then before Sasha had a chance to retort Jasmine turned her back, pressed a kiss on Nathan's cheek and whispered something into his ear.

A colossal lump stuck in Sasha's throat. If these were his friends then she was better off not knowing them. If ever she'd thought she might fit into his life, even for a moment, being hounded by the press outside and then here in this cold, unfriendly space proved she'd been delusional.

But she tilted her chin up and gifted them all the best smile she could muster. Dignifying Jasmine's comments with a response would only aggravate an already tense situation—and she didn't want to embarrass Nate in public. But she sure as heck wouldn't be accompanying him anywhere else.

'Not tonight, Jasmine.' Nate stepped back and fixed an equally plastic smile that did not reach his eyes. The clenched fist at his side was not unnoticed by Sasha.

'Oh? Busy boy? Tomorrow, then. Whenever you're ready, Nate.' *I'll be waiting.* Jasmine didn't say it, but every pore of her eye-lifted-cheek-filled-lip-plumped face screamed, *Take me to bed.* 'Call me.' Then she pressed another kiss on his cheek, leaving a dark red stain.

That kiss said so much. It said, *I know you.* I've had you. I want you again.

It said she was everything Sasha wasn't. Rich, beautiful. Fabulous, with her enhanced face and triple-F chest. It said she knew the ways of Nate's world. How to act, how to be. How to snag her man. And that she could do it, if she wanted. Right now. In fact, she already had.

And then it happened. Shocking and unexpected.

A swirl of frank jealousy that started as a hot blaze on Sasha's cheeks, rushed to her gut, curling her hands round the stem of her glass, and hit her…smack in the chest.

She'd been lured by his heat, by the reluctant kindness hidden underneath that dark-edged womanising mask. By his to-die-for ass. And now she was becoming far too interested in him. And that could never happen. Never. Again.

CHAPTER SIX

CRAZY REALLY, ONE bar, two exes.

One who was all over him like a rash. The other looking as if she'd rather be any place but here.

Nate unwound himself from his ex-fiancée's grip and went over to Miss Nineteen-Fifty-Seven. For all her bravado she hadn't been able to hide the shot of pink to her cheeks with Jasmine's uncharitable line.

Sometimes he hated how shallow everything was. This world that he'd craved, that he loved, that he used just as much as it used him.

But now, because of it, Sasha looked plain miserable sitting at the bar slugging back red wine and nibbling at the deconstructed asparagus crostini. His stomach growling for proper food and his mood seriously dented, Nate yearned for…what? Damned if he knew. But it wasn't this.

'I'm sorry. Jasmine tends to be a little possessive.'

'So I see. I thought I might need a crowbar to prise her off you.' Sasha raised her glass and took another sip. 'She's clearly a very good friend.'

'An old one.'

Friends? Great question, Sasha. He looked around at the mish-mash of celebrities. He knew every one of them—none of them well. He understood how important it was to be seen at events like this, to raise his profile, to sell records, make deals. But he didn't fit in here. He didn't fit the settled life with Jasmine either. He didn't fit in Chesterton. Where on earth did he fit?

He filled his home, hotel rooms, days and nights with employees, groupies, hangers-on, but he always kept a distance, at least emotionally. That was how he liked it. On the outside looking in—that way he could do as he pleased, when he pleased, and had no one to answer to. No one who invested in him or wanted something back.

Sasha grinned. 'She's very…tactile. At school we have a no-contact rule.' Grabbing a tissue, she swiped at the place Jasmine had kissed his cheek. 'That's better—not quite your colour. She'd get a detention with that kind of behaviour.'

'That's Jasmine, breaking all the rules.' He forced out a laugh. But it was far from honest. It was all mixed up with the sudden realisation that, despite how full his timetable was, his life was pretty damned empty.

And then there was that wild disconnected heartbeat Sasha instilled in him…

The things he wanted to do to her—*with* her—as those navy-blue eyes held his gaze, man, things he'd never craved like that before. To get lost in her until he could find himself.

He already knew that was impossible.

'Actually, I've had enough of this place. We should go.'

'So soon? And I was having so much fun.' Relief flooded her face, her voice upbeat, positive energy flowing from her. 'Where to now? What's next in this riveting instalment of your amazing life?'

'Home. I'll drop you off.' He couldn't help stepping closer just to inhale her flowery smell again, willing her optimistic vibe to weave through him.

'Oh. Yes, of course.' She looked taken aback, not affronted exactly, but surprised. 'Looks like it's sausages for one, then, after all.'

As she leaned forward to pick up her bag he caught a glimpse of lace, creamy flesh, breasts that looked just about perfect. Before he had the chance to tear his gaze away her head dipped back up, and she caught him looking, heat hitting her pupils.

Home sounded like a very good idea. Hers. Now. He failed to swallow the question forming on his tongue. 'How about sausages for two? Catch up on old times?' *Make some new ones too*?

As she wiped her hands on the napkin her eyes grew wide. 'You want to come back to my place? For sausages? That's…novel. No one's ever asked me to do that before.'

'No? Then, Sasha, hold onto your hat. I may even cook.' At the thought of being alone with her his groin tightened.

'Really? Don't you have people to do that for you?' Her lips parted just enough, the quick dart of her tongue to moisten lipstick-free lips. Wet. Hot…

'There are some things I have people for. And some things I really much prefer to do myself.'

Where was he going with this? The last few days had been like an ancient dance, pulling together, parting, touching and stepping away. How easy it would be to crank up the tempo and take it to its logical conclusion.

Easy and pretty stupid to have even one kiss with the woman who had pushed him to his limits years ago.

But his mouth and brain had total disconnect. 'Your place would be much more private.'

'I don't want you getting the wrong idea. Sausages and mashed potatoes—that's all that's on offer. Seriously. Nothing more. So don't even think it.' She swung down from the bar stool and fiddled with her dress, flashed a wry smile. When she spoke again her voice was hoarse and warm. 'You'll have to leave Tweedle Dum and your ego at the door. There's just not enough room. It's the size of a shoebox.'

'Excellent, cosy. Even better. Let's go.' The feel of her

soft hand as it fitted into his sent shivers through him. 'Brace yourself for the cameras again. This isn't going to be pretty. Stick with me.'

Opening the door to a cacophony of camera shutters, Nate dipped his head and focused on the pavement ahead, told her to do the same. Business as usual for him, but she looked scared to death.

A wave of irritation rippled through him as, for a moment, he wished he could shield her from the ugly side of fame.

'Nate!' one of the photographers yelled over as if he were his friend. 'Where are you going to now? Trudy's, Opal? Who's your friend?'

'Mind your own business.' Shoving past them down the street, he tried to decide which direction to follow. 'There's no car.' In his hurry to leave he'd completely overlooked that.

She rolled her eyes. 'Tube? Taxi? Bus? Like normal people. Oh, sorry, I forgot, you're not normal.'

'Tube? Do you have any idea…?' No, she didn't. 'We'll walk until we see a black cab. The trick is to keep moving.' The photographers followed, clicking and whirring, shouting and clamouring. 'Welcome to the greatest show on earth. My private life.'

'It's like being in a zoo.' She grimaced as she tripped over a guy who had his lens in her face. Her eyes flickered with fear as she tried to hide her face. 'Ouch, sorry.'

'Don't apologise to them.' He shouldn't have cajoled her into coming here, knowing how much she liked to play safe. His heart twisting at what he was prepared to put her through for his own needs, Nate came to a halt, put his hand on the man's chest. 'Leave us alone, mate. It's a private night out.'

'Nate, it's fine.' Biting down on her lip, she looked even

more alarmed at his reaction than the gross intrusion of privacy. 'Please, leave it. It's not worth it.'

Maybe they weren't, but she was. The camera jutted into her face. His irritation turned hot.

'I mean it, *mate*.' Nate's hands curled instinctively as he wished he hadn't made that vow ten years ago: that he would never hit another human being again. But, God, the feel of his knuckle against that man's jaw would be sweet right now.

His shoulders ratcheted back as he leaned towards them all, tried to rein in his anger. 'I said leave us alone or I'll slap you with a lawsuit so quick you won't have time to put your lens cap on. Get outta here.'

As one the group stopped moving. They didn't retreat, but they didn't take another step forward either. And the clicking and whirring stopped.

'Nathan.' Sasha's face had leeched of colour and her hand shook against his arm. 'Please.'

He drew her a few more feet away from the photographers and lowered his voice. 'Sasha, listen to me, they'll follow us for ever. Don't you understand?'

No? Hell if he did either.

This need to protect her—where had it come from? And why so intense? It made no sense. Ten years ago, maybe, but not now. Why did she bring out that primal instinct in him when he thought he was through with it?

'No, I don't understand, Nathan. Not at all.' Her gaze was hard as it clashed with his. 'Next time you fancy a fight, don't invite me.'

'What is this?'

She scowled. 'You know I hate this…violence. And yet, here you are showing off or something with your fists. It… it scares me.'

'Hell.' The truth hit him square in the gut. He was acting no better than his own useless father, lashing out and angry. Again. 'I'm sorry. You know I'd never do anything to hurt you.'

'Yeah—?' Turning away she suddenly careered forward into the road, her foot buckling under her. He grabbed out, caught her as she plunged towards the concrete. Next thing he knew he was holding her, his chest frozen with fear of what might have happened. Because of his stupid feral overreaction. 'Are you okay?'

'I stumbled, that's all.' She shook out of his arms. 'For goodness' sake, I can manage. I'm not some stupid hapless woman.'

'No. I can see that.' He turned her by the shoulder to face him. 'But I'm just not prepared to share you with them.'

'So you act like an animal instead? All hot-headed, shoot first? Have you not learnt a thing?'

'Of course I have. I've been living with the choices I made for the last decade.'

But this was different, he was different. He could contain the rage now. He just couldn't contain the passion that fed it. Didn't want to. He wanted to feel things, didn't want to become the empty carcass that the shrink's uppers and downers had made him following Marshall's death. 'I'm not allowed to get angry? To feel things? Is that right?'

'Of course you can feel things. But making a fuss will clearly make it worse.' Under his fingers tension rippled through her body, but heat hit her eyes. 'You can't get so… passionate about things like this. You have to control yourself.'

As she did. Sasha had always tried to control every nuance of emotion to the point it had almost driven him crazy. 'I understand I have to tolerate it. There are times I happily walk that line—I even enjoy it. Don't get me wrong, I love the fame, the money, the whole thing. But not today… And not with you.'

'Oh.' Blinking once. Twice. Three times, she opened

her mouth to say more, then obviously decided not to. The hand she held to his chest trembled. But bingo, the heat was returning to those eyes. 'Then why didn't you just say so?'

'You were too busy tearing a strip off me. And I was too busy being a jerk.'

Mouth pursed, she shook her head and tutted. 'Finally he says something sensible.'

'Finally she shuts up long enough to let him. Can you walk?'

'I think so.' She nodded as he wrapped an arm round her waist.

'Then let's get out of here.'

Streetlights flickered into life as the sky darkened, mirroring his mood. As they walked thunderous black clouds blocked the last dying rays of the sun. Thick drops began to fall, slowly at first in a kind of staccato waltz, getting faster and thicker. Good old London in the spring.

Zigzagging through the dark west London streets they finally lost the photographers and lost themselves in the process.

She pushed her palms onto his chest. 'Great one. My shoes are ruined. My foot hurts…This has got to be the best—'

'Let's just take a minute to get our bearings.' He dragged her out of the rain into a shop doorway; bedraggled hair dripped onto her shoulders. Her dress stuck to her, delineating her shape, the tight swell of her breasts, the dip of her waist. Black streaks ran down both cheeks. And yes, normally he'd walk past a woman like her—but just seeing her all fired up made his heart race erratically and his body harden.

'Fine. Great. I'm already soaked to the skin, take as long as you—'

But before she could say another word he grabbed her

wrist, gently now, pinned her against the shop door. 'God, you're beautiful.'

'And you're an idiot.'

'Doing this, here, probably. But I can't help it.'

His arms curled round her waist, brought her closer. Her breasts pressed against his chest, her lips parted just enough for him to feel her warm breath on his face. Heat engulfed him, a fierce need that meshed with the anger at those stupid trolls and the ache to kiss her.

No—his anger dissipated as quickly as it had come. And the gaping hole that was left was filled with her.

The heavy bass beat from the club opposite blurred out of focus; his peripheral vision turned to fuzz. All he could see were huge blue eyes staring up at him, telling him what he needed to know. She felt it too, this wild crazy buzz. And she had no idea what to do with it either.

Careless and foolish to want her here in such a public place, but all he could think of was tasting those lips, feeling her righteous anger and uncertainty and downright sweetness in his arms. And sometimes, just sometimes he regretted courting the publicity that had made him such a success. Sometimes he wished he could live a normal life where no one cared who he kissed.

His thumb tracked to her lip but she didn't move, didn't blink, just kept on staring up at him with eyes that swirled with the same messed-up emotions as he had in his gut.

'Sasha.' He tilted his head towards her, saw the flicker of doubt, but he'd already seen the heat and knew she was fighting it too. 'God, I want you and I can't stop.'

'We have to stop.'

'Really? Do we? No one can see us—it's just you and me.'

She nodded. 'But, what next?'

He rested his forehead against hers. 'I don't know. We'll deal with it.' Somehow.

But when her tongue darted out and licked her bottom lip he was gone. Lost. Flailing around in the essence of her, looking for something to grasp onto. But the only thing that could anchor him was her.

Slanting his mouth over hers, he dipped his head and pressed his lips against the corner of her mouth. He felt her stuttered breath, the jolt of electricity that simultaneously rocked their bodies. And drank in the taste of oranges and stark clear honesty.

He knew this was insane and then some, starting something he could never follow through on. Not the way she'd want him to. It was the craziest messed-up thing he'd ever done—and that was pushing it.

But damn it, he wanted to forget what was right or wrong. Especially when it felt so good.

Oh, hell.

Nate's hands cupped her face, his light nibbles on her bottom lip sending a thousand shots of desire skittering through her, to her back, to her legs, and low down where an ache spread keen and unyielding.

Angling his head closer, he pressed his lips full onto her mouth, eliciting a groan from her throat that was deep and feral and hungry.

It wasn't the clumsy kiss of a teenager as she remembered.

It was the kiss of a man, mature, experienced, unlike her. His hands tangled in her hair, ran down her back, cupping her bottom as the kiss deepened. His tongue gently teased against hers, each stroke making her lose another grip on reality. Making her give in to dangerous temptation; just once. Then she would go back to her nice safe life where passion was a distant memory. Something other people did.

Madness, though, to be doing this with the man who had

taught her how love could make you soar, and how much it could hurt, and who had the capacity to do it all over again.

Nate was a man of sharp contrasts and driven by passion, but he wasn't going to stick around. And he certainly wouldn't suit a nice sensible car and slippers.

But by God, he was divine.

Snaking her arms around his neck, she pulled him closer. Through his jeans she felt his hardness push against her, showing her just how much he wanted her. And that knowledge seemed to suck the air away between them. Her nipples beaded against his chest; heat pooled in her gut.

Resisting him was hard enough in the daylight, but having him wrapped around her, damp and hot and hard in the dark, was testing her to the limits. He wanted her.

And she wanted him right back. Wanted to feel him, taste him, touch him. A desperate ache tugged at her abdomen as she groaned, imagining how he would feel deep inside her.

No.

She caught her breath as waves of panic rolled through her. She fought for air.

'Stop. Stop.' Turning away from him, she breathed in the spicy smells and the dull thick sounds of the suburb, waited until her heart rate slowed. 'I'm sorry, Nathan. I've told you before—this isn't a game.'

He shook his head, desire and confusion lodged in the dark shadows of his face. 'And I wasn't playing you, Sasha. This wasn't what I planned.'

'And what exactly did you plan?'

'You want a list? Really? Bullet points? I don't know! I'm not like you. I don't plan every single move.'

Yes, and Plan A had been lost somewhere in the depths of his mind-numbing kiss. 'Maybe you should. I definitely should. This can't go anywhere. We're too different—our lives are poles apart.'

He seemed to be trying to shake off the bad mood that had descended. 'We could just have some fun?'

'No. I don't do fun.' Not fun in the sense he meant, because that kind of fun wasn't lasting, or sensible. How to admit that, sexually, she wasn't much more experienced than the last time he'd kissed her? He'd laugh in her face. 'And that sounds so hopelessly sad.'

'Yes. It does.' The moment very definitely deflated, he looked out of the shop front as a yellow light illuminated the street. Grabbing her hand, he pulled her to the kerb and waved. 'A cab. Quick. Let's do something fun, then, shake things up. Where should we go? Brighton? Paris? Edinburgh? New York? Anywhere you want.'

Bed? Maybe she could deal with it now. It had been a long time since she'd tried.

To be honest, the geography didn't matter, but the reality did. 'Oh, sure, I'm all into a spontaneous trip when I have school tomorrow. In the real world people work nine to five. You take it, I'm fine—the tube station's bound to be round here somewhere.' She just needed to get away from him before she was bamboozled into something else, something even more dangerous.

Even in this light she could see the frown and the concern. 'Are you mad? Do you know this area?'

'Not really, not in the dark. But I'll be fine—it's only Portobello.'

'Exactly. You are not wandering the streets on your own. Whatever happened to Miss Safe and Sensible?'

Great question—she'd been wondering that herself. 'Seems she's had a day off, but she's back now and she wants to go home.' On her own.

CHAPTER SEVEN

'CERTIFIABLE. OUT OF your mind bonkers. Deranged. Gaga. Loony. No sister of mine. No sir-ee. You left sex-on-a-stick and went home in a cab? If you don't watch out you'll end up a lonely crazy cat lady.' Cassie's incredulous voice crackled through Sasha's mobile phone as she killed time in the hall between school ending and rehearsals beginning.

Seven days, twelve hours and thirty-five minutes later and her sister still wouldn't let the Nate subject drop. 'I need more details. He was good? Great? The best?'

'All of the above. And I don't have a cat.' She tried for the elder-sister voice but ended up sounding cross. Truth was, she always regretted telling Cassie anything about her private life because she only used it as a rod to beat her with. A sad, pathetic rod dented with a history of lies and let-downs. Safe men, she'd discovered, didn't always look after your heart.

And now this. A spectacularly failed attempt at living dangerously.

Page five in the gossip rags. Albeit a grainy photo of her falling over; no one would even recognise it was her. But Nathan's snarly expression had peered out, accompanied by the usual gory story about his unstable rocky lifestyle.

So she should stay well clear. She didn't want to risk being identified and all the stress that would bring to her family. But the man wouldn't leave her head alone.

'It's only a matter of time, Sash. Before you know it you'll find a cute stray kitten and bring it home…and another to keep it company, and another. Then knitting will suddenly seem really fun, making jam, crocheted toilet-roll holders… It's a slippery slope to spinsterdom.'

'I'm twenty-seven—there's plenty of time to find my soul mate. And people don't say spinster any more. Or *on the shelf.* Smart women choose life partners carefully. They don't jump into bed with the first offer.'

'But they do jump into bed with someone at some point. You need to get laid or you'll be spinster central. You'll have spinster parties. Go on spinster holidays.' Sasha held the phone away from her ear as her irritating sibling continued her tirade. Which, unfortunately, was a hard smack of truth she didn't need to hear.

She'd waited a long time for Mr Right, and he seemed strangely reluctant to show up. Just her luck the only man who'd shown any interest was part gigolo, part magician. One word from him and her common sense had disappeared in a puff of smoke.

'…You can be Queen Spinster. All hail Empress Sasha Spinster the—'

'Okay, okay. Enough already. Do we really need to talk about my sex life?'

'You haven't got one. Sash…' The soft edge to her sister's voice made Sasha wince. 'It's been such a long time. It might be different. You should try again. You just need the right man…and why not Nate?'

'Yes, well…' She would not have a conversation about her sexual inadequacy over the telephone. 'Not everyone wants dirty sex up against a doorway. Even if it is with Mr Obnoxious himself.'

'Oh, really? How disappointing.' The deep voice came from behind Sasha, dark and dangerous and loaded with teasing.

It was perilously close to her ear lobe, and that sensitive spot at the back of her neck, which fired on full alert sparking lust hormones to break out from every pore. 'So where *would* you like dirty sex, Sasha? Because I'm happy to oblige, any time. My jet is on standby. Just say the word.'

Oh. My. God. *Do not turn around. Do not turn around.* Her heart drummed as she winced and overheated at the same time. A shiver of need tore through her body at the mere sound of his voice. That kiss marked a line that they'd crossed, and while her body thrummed her head ached to jump right back to safety.

She fumbled for the phone volume control and hissed, 'Cassie, I have to go.'

'Why? Rehearsals don't start for ten more minutes, so we have plenty of time to run through the details again. Okay. Slowly. From the top…Rain. Doorway. Lips. Tongues? Oh…you wanted him. Oh…he was so gorgeous. But you just couldn't—'

'Shut. Up.'

The wide smug grin that hit her in the face as she turned round to face Nate told her he'd heard. Every single belittling word. She closed her eyes, shook her head and rued the day she'd coached Cassie to speak clearly and loudly for her drama practical exam.

And judging by his smile it seemed Nathan agreed with her sister: a little seeing-to wouldn't go amiss. Why pass up on the chance of some fun? Life was too short, and all that gumbo people used to excuse bad behaviour.

But she'd kissed that smiling mouth. And it had been good. Very, very good. So good the intense tingling through her body had driven her wild ever since. So she could see they had a point. 'Someone's here, Cassie. I've got to go.'

'Who? Oh, your voice. It's changed. Soft, hoarse. Come-to-bed…' Her sister laughed. 'It's him. Isn't it? Nate's there…at the school?'

Prising the phone gently from her hand, Nathan smiled. Wearing his usual uniform of black with black and a dash of…black, he looked lip-smackingly devastatingly beautiful.

A fragile invisible thread pulled her towards him, tugging tighter and tighter. It had started to tense the moment her eyes locked with his in the men's room and now felt so taut it would snap at any moment.

Struggling for breath, she handed her phone over.

'Cassie? Nate here.' He held the phone away from his ear as she squealed. 'Your sister has to go now. We have some…unfinished business to attend to.'

Not bloody likely. Sasha winced again. Seven days, twelve hours and twenty minutes ago she'd made the decision to never look at him with sex on her mind again. To not talk to him unless for purely professional purposes. To not breathe in that gorgeous smell that made her legs weak and her head woozy.

Oops. Too late.

That had been one hell of a kiss.

Long and hard. It had stoked a fierce need in him. And Nate wanted to do it again. Now.

What Nate wanted, Nate always got.

But not Sasha. And that was the biggest bounce his ego had taken in a long time, so much so he'd come back for more. Against all better judgement and Dario's protestations. Strange what frank hot-blooded lust could do to a man.

Two hours of immersing himself in choir rehearsals and he still couldn't take his eyes off her, off the wide-legged trousers and floaty top with a plunging flouncy neckline that gave him enough glimpse of her breasts to strain for more. Couldn't forget how she'd felt in his arms, how she'd wanted that kiss as much as he had. He'd seen it brimming in her eyes, felt it in her body's response.

And, okay, she'd been right to end it. Having seen the salacious photos in the paper he knew his most sensible course of action was to leave her alone.

Harsh truth: he couldn't give her what she wanted. He didn't do relationships; flings yes, togetherness, no. He preferred keeping a distance, not making promises; the only connection he enjoyed was physical. And Sasha was definitely the all-or-nothing fairy-tale melding-of-souls kind of woman.

So it was a good thing he wouldn't see her again after the concert.

Wasn't it?

She walked towards him, heels tapping across the parquet floor, her floral scent drifting around him and drawing him closer, firing all his senses on full alert.

'Once again you've come to the rescue and made the performances so much stronger. You know so much about creating a good show, theatrics, stage presence…everything. The kids really react well to your tuition, Nathan. You're a good teacher.'

'Nah. They're good at listening.' But the swell of pride in his chest left little room for oxygen. He'd spent so much of his time working on his performances, his career, his spectacularly colourful downtime, he hadn't had the chance to think how he might be able to help others. Until now, and it felt surprisingly good.

Sasha had packed everything away apart from a thick wad of large posters in her hand, which she showed him, delight emanating from her erect posture and eager eyes. 'Do you like these? I've sent them to the local radio stations and I'm going to put them in the shop windows in the mall.'

'Wow. They're good.' Artfully crafted and bright enough to catch anyone's eye. 'But can you make my name smaller?

Less bold? It's a shame to have it dominating the line-up when the kids have done all the work.'

'You don't like it?' She seemed deflated. 'We thought we'd sell more tickets if we put you centre. You seem to make headlines whatever you do.'

'Not everyone has the same bouncy positivity you have. I did warn you it would be ugly.'

She shook her head and held up a finger. 'Okay. Well, let's put the other night completely behind us. I've forgotten it already. We need to focus forward on getting those kids to the competition. That's what this is about.'

Forget it? He'd come running back for more.

But she was right, this wasn't about him or that kiss, it was about kids like Marshall. 'How many tickets have you sold?'

'None as yet. I have to collect them from the printers now, on my way to the shops.' Glancing at her watch, she said, 'Oops…before they close.'

'You made the posters. You collect the tickets. You do the drop-offs. Is there no one else to help?'

'Are you offering?'

No way.

At his hesitation she laughed, resignedly. 'I thought not. The kids helped with the poster design and they're all taking tickets home to sell door-to-door. But I said I'd do this. And no, there is no one else to help, Nathan. And that's absolutely fine.'

'I could get someone to do it for you.' That would get the job done without getting his hands dirty, and his head even more messed up by being with her longer than was good for him. 'You know, you work too hard.'

'Says Mr My-job-is-my-life. If I do it I know the information has been given correctly. I'm invested in this. I can't risk someone else making a mess of it.'

'It's a poster, for a kids' show. What mess could they

make? They stick it in a window, with tape.' But okay, he got it. She took her job and her responsibilities very seriously. She was dedicated and ambitious. He respected her drive and attention to detail—even if it did get bloody annoying at times. That, and the fact she was an out-of-control control freak, meant she had to do the donkey work. On her own.

He followed her out into the afternoon sunshine, tried hard not to look at the way the light silhouetted her shapely legs through the flimsy trousers.

Suddenly the thought of her walking the littered grimy streets for those needy kids made his heart ache. 'You want some company?'

What the...?

'No, Nathan. Please don't.' She came to an abrupt halt and looked up at him, doubt and uncertainty swimming in her eyes. Shoulders hiked again around her ears.

'Don't what?'

A muscle in her jaw tensed and he suspected she was biting back what she really wanted to say. 'Don't be kind to me.'

That was a label no one had pinned on him before. 'Whoa, Sasha, no. That wasn't my intention. I was more concerned that the publicity machine cranks into action sooner rather than later. There's only a week to go and I refuse to perform to a half-filled house. You dawdling here chewing the fat isn't getting the job done. But it's okay, do it on your own. Take as long as you like. Fine.'

'Great.' Her eyes rolled. 'You give, and then you take away. Typical.'

'Now I'm the bad guy?'

'Nathan, you're always the bad guy.'

Figures. And he was well and truly backed into a corner. 'I won't try to kiss you again, if that's what you're worried about. Although, I am going to think about it. A lot.'

The shoulders relaxed a little and a hint of a smile played over her lips. 'Thinking I don't particularly care about. Acting is definitely a no-no. There are way too many shop fronts out there. We'd never get any of these posters delivered. Just so you know, and in case you're in any way confused about the issue—kissing is not going to happen again.'

'And there was me thinking you'd forgotten all about it.' So the kiss had been eating her. It had eaten away at him too, but now he just ached for more. And she clearly… didn't. 'Okay. No kissing. You have my word.'

'Good. Definitely.' She chewed the corner of her lip and he wanted to smother those lips all over again. Wanted to explore other parts of her body too. Heat zipped through his veins.

Leaning closer, he whispered in her ear, 'Are you trying to convince me? Or yourself?'

'You. I'm already well and truly convinced. So it's good you understand. Good. Brilliant. Fabulous. No kissing.' She glanced towards the street. 'Er…no one's lurking in the shadows. Are you on your own today? Tweedle Dum gone rogue?'

'I gave Dario the afternoon off. Is that so strange?' Yup. Dario had certainly thought so, seeing as they usually spent pretty much every waking moment together.

But since that doorway kiss Nate hadn't been able to focus on anything, certainly not on scheduling another tour or a round of TV interviews to promote his new album. Couldn't stand being cooped up in an office. Didn't want to be outside. Couldn't bear listening to Dario's retorts about getting too serious about a bunch of kids going nowhere.

Driving around had done nothing to salve his unease. Suddenly he'd found himself back here. Fuelled by lust. No plan, as always. As she said. Rushing headlong into danger, and meeting disaster along the way. 'This gig has my name on it—it's got to work or I look lame. I just wanted to see how rehearsals were going. He didn't. So I came solo.'

'Okay…well, you're here now and it's getting late.' She handed him a roll of tape. 'Put your money where your big mouth is and get sticking. But don't expect a heap of excitement. It's only Chesterton, and you know what that's like.' Her voice was breathy, trying to be nonchalant. 'It'll be dull and dreary.'

It was far from that. Other than having to stop every five minutes for Sasha to speak to a friend, a neighbour, a parent of a pupil, a colleague, they managed a lot of laughs and convinced fifteen shopkeepers to display her poster.

'No one's recognised you yet. Great disguise today, by the way.'

'I guess no one expects Nate Munro to be ambling down the high street.' He pulled the hoodie more tightly over his head, and pushed the aviator shades back, blending in with the other guys milling around.

Nothing had changed. Sure, the hardware store was now a one-pound shop, the butchers had closed down, more estate agents, a couple of different burger bars, the feel was still very much rundown and shabby. Just as he remembered.

But the sun glinted off the windows; people smiled as they walked by; it was shabby with hope. And that hadn't been there ten years ago. At least he'd never seen it. But he'd been so engulfed by his own private war that he hadn't been able to see past his fists and his anger.

Maybe if he'd looked outside instead of dwelling on the inner pain he'd have made fewer devastating mistakes and even stayed a little longer. Who knew what his life would have been like then? Would he have married Sasha as she'd planned? Would he have ordinary friends he could trust instead of people trampling over him to get what they wanted?

Would he have saved Marshall?

Would Marshall have even *needed* saving? That, he didn't want to think about.

She stopped outside a quaint-looking Italian restaurant. Painted bright red with chipped wooden shutters, windows dressed with café-style net curtains, it looked as if it had been uprooted from Nate's favourite Italian village and plonked down in south London. 'This place has the best pasta in town. Do you want to come in and wait while I talk to lovely Luigi? He's bound to want to help the choir—he's always such a good supporter of the school.'

'Lovely Luigi?'

The spike of jealousy that erupted from nowhere must have shown on his face, because she smiled and shoved her hands on her waist. 'The owner. He's about a hundred.'

No man from the age of five upwards would be blind to Sasha's sunny sensual appeal. He wasn't going to take any chances. 'Believe me, sweet thing, it doesn't matter what age they are, if they've got it, they'll use it.'

'Oh, I can manage. I usually fight all those hordes of men off with a stick. But I guess today you'll have to do. Be nice.'

'Aren't I always?'

'No.'

Within seconds they were ensconced at a table with a background of soft lilting opera music. Rather, Nate was ensconced, alone, while Sasha's attention was held at the bar by three elderly Italian men. One stared into her eyes and smiled inanely. One poured her a drink of *prosecco*, and Luigi, the elderly patriarch, brought her little tidbits of food to try from the kitchen.

Eventually she meandered over with two glasses of wine and handed him one, her eyes bright. 'That's eight tickets sold. They're all aware of who you are and they've sworn not to tell a soul that you're here. And they would be honoured to bring you some food, if you have the time.'

Not really but he'd make an exception. He kind of liked the comfortable feel of the place, with no one pressing for his attention or fawning over him. Shucking the hoodie over his head he relaxed into relative anonymity. 'I'd be honoured to eat it. I love Italian food.'

'Me too.' She sat opposite him and ran her hands over the dark green plastic tablecloth. 'I've been saving to go on a trip to Italy one day. Luigi has given me lists of all the best things to do and how to discover the places where the locals eat in Florence and Siena. Apparently they're a well-kept secret.'

'You just need to know who to ask. Usually a bit of grappa works as a bribe.'

'You seem to know a lot about it. Have you been to Italy?' She laughed. 'Stupid question, really, you've probably been everywhere and I must seem like a Hicksville country cousin.'

'There's nothing Hicksville about living in South London. It's more like the wild west. I'm sure you'll get to Italy one day, Sasha. Of all the people I know, you are the one who always achieved what she set out to do.' Without any cut-throat, malicious back-stabbing too. She manoeuvred with ease, making sure everyone else was comfortable and safe too, rather than grasping for what she wanted, regardless. 'You just haven't had the breaks I've had. I've been very lucky to travel the world. Even if I did see most of it from a hotel window.'

'Well, Italy's on my bucket list. It would be a perfect start, especially if they have food like this.' She tore off a piece of bread, offered it to him so naturally, as if caring and nurturing ran in her blood. His heart snagged at the tender gesture. Some guy would be lucky to have her as a wife. A family. She completed that picture.

But not for him. He hadn't been joking when he'd said marriage would be the kiss of death to his career. To his privacy. To the steel he'd constructed around his heart.

He found her a smile of thanks, dipped the bread in a dish of thick dark green olive oil and ate it. It was perfect rustic ciabatta, the like of which he'd only ever had in his local village. The place he told no one about, the only sanctuary he had away from the madness.

And yet suddenly the words were spilling from his lips. 'I have a place in Tuscany. Unfortunately I don't get to visit very often. I haven't been for a couple of years, what with the tour, filming…' He neglected to tell her he'd had plans to go next week, but had cancelled them for her concert. There would be other times.

After swallowing her bread, she cleared her delicate throat, took a sip of the light sparkling wine. 'Aren't you more the party-animal type? Isn't Ibiza more your thing?'

'It was.' He shrugged, suppressing a smile at the chaos of party central and his part in its rise in popularity amongst the celebrity set. 'For a while. Until I got kicked out.'

'Really? Why am I not surprised?' Watching the innocent shock in her eyes was pure delight.

He laughed and felt the warm relaxation that only decent food and good company could bring. Something that had been missing from his life for too long. When he got back to Malibu he was definitely sacking the chef. Too much raw organic food made a man go quietly insane.

'I had a few more-than-wild parties, caused some damage. They wanted to ban me but I make them far too much cash. Mind you, they have to spend a lot too. Driving cars into pools takes some paying for.' He leaned back in his chair, stretched his legs under the table. 'I'm getting just a little tired of that.'

Her brows knotted. 'Nate Munro tired of partying? Is the world coming to an end? What will the papers be full of now? Proper news?'

'Hey, I'm just a little bored of the same old scene, on the lookout for something new, the next big thing. I'm not ready for my pipe and slippers yet.'

'Slippers. Ah, yes. Somehow I just can't see you in woolly tartan.' The smile she gave him was gentle and wistful, as if she was enjoying her own private joke. 'So, tell me about the delightful Jasmine.'

He didn't want to talk about himself, and definitely not about Jasmine. He wanted to find out about Sasha, what made her tick now, what she liked to do. Just listening to her sweet soft voice soothed his aching head.

And watching her mouth as she talked almost drove him mad with desire. Each moment he didn't touch her was a study in self-control. But he was running out. Fast.

'My ex? My wannabe wife. Nothing to say really. She subscribes to the take, take, take, mantra. She always wants more. And it's never enough.' Or he wasn't enough. Jasmine had thrown back at him one too many times that he was missing the human connection gene. *You have to give a little, Nate.* Seemed she didn't just mean his credit card. 'We dated, moved in together for a while. Then she left me, fleeced me but I'm still her fall-back guy, should her master plan to hook an even more rich and famous sucker not work out.'

The little frown lining Sasha's forehead dipped. 'And yet you smile and talk to her like she's so important to you.'

'She's Dario's little sister. I have to show respect.'

'Ah.'

'It's complicated.'

'Is there anything about you that isn't?'

'Probably not. Things get incestuous out there. Everyone's connected to somebody. Or wants to be. Or tries to be.' He grinned at her rapid blink. 'A long time ago Dario helped me when I needed someone. Upshot is, I owe him a lot.' And now he'd said way too much about his private life and still knew nothing about hers. But that was her through and through: she gave a little, but never quite enough. Now, why did that have a familiar ring to it? 'What about you?'

'Me? Oh, I don't owe Dario anything.'

He snorted into his wine. 'Be gentle with me, Sasha. That sharp wit could pierce a man's heart. You know what I mean—what about your life?'

'Oh, okay.' She winked. 'Let me think…I have no minder, no significant ex who fleeced me. I have no houses in Italy and the States…'

'No boyfriend? Husband? Secret baby?'

'If I told you about the baby, it wouldn't be secret then, would it?' At his frown she shrugged. 'Okay, there's no baby.'

'And husband?'

'Ah…' Waving her hand nonchalantly she flashed a serene smile. 'Number one was lovely but secretly gay, but we had a lot of fun shopping. Number two…' She sighed and put a hand to her chest. 'Tragic. Number three—'

'Wait! What? Number three?'

'Come on, Nate. Please. I have no babies. No husbands, ex or otherwise. This is Chesterton not California. And this is me, Sasha, schoolteacher, not your average pack-a-whole-lifetime-in-before-you're-twenty-one Hollywood starlet. After you left town I finished school, went to uni. I haven't found Mr Right yet—he's strangely elusive. Or maybe I'm just too picky.'

'Well, that's a relief.'

'Why?'

Yeah. Why? It was none of his business who she'd slept with or what her marriage plans were. But for some reason he wanted to kick her Mr Right into touch. 'You're far too young to settle down.'

She shot him a look of amusement. 'You need to talk to Cassie then. She thinks I'm over the hill and that I need to find a husband quick, before I get too old and no one would want me.'

How could anyone not want her? The V in her top drew his gaze. Tiny pearl buttons ran over the swell of her breasts and he wondered how easy it would be to pop them open. One. By. One. And once undone, what would he find underneath? Lace? Silk?

His brain filled with a sexual haze. His voice was rough as he spoke. 'Well, make sure you don't rush into anything. Take your time.'

'What? Relationship advice, from you? That's a hoot.' She laughed. 'But don't fret, I'm never one to rush into things. I like to take things slow and steady. You probably think my life is deathly boring but I like it.'

Boring? Most definitely not, but he knew her well enough not to push the subject. Sasha had lived through more trauma than most other people he knew. Her father's suicide had been a bolt out of the blue, which she always flatly refused to talk about. It was only when other friends had mentioned it at school that he'd found out. Even then, the details had been sketchy. That she hadn't trusted him enough to confide had bitten hard. 'Hey, it's your life, live it how you like. I do.'

'And we all know how well that works out. Meanwhile, I stick to my life plan.' Her mouth tipped into a smile that he wanted to taste.

Kissing her would be very bad. And so damned good. But he'd promised. 'But it is such a waste.'

'Of what?'

'All that brain-power spent on graphs and spread-sheets. So...linear and neat and ordered. When you could

be thinking up ways to spend your time more…messily…'
He leaned closer, watched the flush on her cheeks, imagined her breathless and spent in his bed, her legs wrapped
round him. 'Messy is good. Messy is better than good. I
could show you some time.'

'Er…no thanks. I'm busy…For ever.' She coughed mid-
fluster, tapping her hand against her cheek, the composed
act failing. She was anything but. How easy would it be
to strip her back to the hot woman he'd had in his arms on
the edge of dirty sex? 'Then, once I qualified I came back
here, got my job at Chesterton High and bought my small
but perfectly formed flat in the new development on Fair-
lie Street. I've come full circle.'

'In more ways than one.' He smiled at her confusion as
his fingertips brushed against hers. A shot of electricity
shot through him as skin met skin. 'You. Me. Us.'

She withdrew her hand immediately, leaving a cold
breath of air in its wake. 'Oh, no. No, Nate. Please, don't
even think that. There can't be any *us*.'

CHAPTER EIGHT

BRILLIANT. NATE'S STOMACH plummeted. *Good shot, Mr Superstar.*

He'd met presidents and royalty, given speeches and interviews, but had never been tongue-tied by a school-teacher before.

'Don't get the wrong impression.' Now she'd think he was a nut-job with his spectacular slip of the tongue. 'I meant, it's funny us sitting here in a café in Chesterton after all these years…'

'I see.' She didn't look convinced. And neither was he. He was rattled. He didn't do this. Assumptions, jealousy, possession. What was happening to him?

Before he could explain further Luigi interrupted with plates laden with antipasto, delicious bite-sized chunks of artichokes, glistening plump olives, spicy salami, salty pro-sciutto. And a jug of dark earthy *chianti classico*. More aromas of garlic and herbs spilled from the kitchen, elemental and sensual. Now he'd have to stick around and worm his way out of embarrassment.

'Eat. Eat. Please,' Luigi pleaded as he fussed around them, squeezing his large belly between the tables. 'There is more coming for my new friend, Nate Munro. And bella Sasha.'

Bella Sasha. That was her in a nutshell. Beautiful. Confident in her own space, and modest. She even had the ancient Luigi eating out of her hand.

'There is one thing, though.' She leaned forward, her words hesitant, as if she was trying to work out the right thing to say. 'I'd like to talk to you about Marshall, to say how sorry I was about his death. I heard from one of your mum's neighbours, and then I heard about her death a few weeks later too. I wanted to send something or to write to you, even go to their funerals, but everything was so private and I didn't want to impose. Marshall was such a joy to know. Everyone loved him.'

Not everyone. But Nate didn't want to go into that now. Regardless of how Sasha made him feel, wanting her in his bed was very different from trusting her with the part of his heart he kept sealed off. The image he'd carefully constructed to keep everyone from knowing the real Nate Munro was too ingrained in him now.

But he could give her a little. Any more than that and he didn't know if he'd be able to stop. 'Yeah. It was a difficult time. If only I...'

She frowned. 'What do you mean? What happened?'

Too late. Pain twisted inside him. 'Nothing.'

A fraught silence hovered between them as she waited for him to explain. When he didn't, she sighed. 'It's okay, I get the picture—you hurt too much. You must miss him terribly.'

He could be upfront about this at least. 'I do. It's like an ache that doesn't go away.'

He'd landed a kid in Intensive Care, lost the respect of his school, the love of his girlfriend, and then the life of his beloved brother and mother. All because he'd had a stupid inflated sense of self-belief.

'Hey, but I certainly mourned them in spectacular fashion. That self-destruct button jammed hard and fast, taking every cliché to excess: wine, women. And the songs.

Introspective and pathetic.' Shrugging, he laughed. 'Gotta love that minor key.'

'But heartfelt and eerily haunting. Truthful.'

'It doesn't matter. It won't right all the wrongs—it won't change the decisions I made, the stupid stuff. It won't bring him back.' The stab to his heart was tight and sharp.

'If it's any consolation, I know how you feel, Nate. It's like…like a light has gone out in your soul.'

For a second his mask almost slipped as he looked up and saw the tears swimming in her eyes. Her hand touched his as she fought to control the wobbling lip. His hurt was all mixed up with the loss of her father.

And he fought to breathe through the weight pressing in on his chest. He didn't do this. Open Pandora's box and let his emotions out, not when he had no idea how to shut them off again without a struggle.

He needed to get out before he hit that self-destruct button again, and dragged beautiful, innocent Sasha down with him.

Scraping the chair back, he stood. 'I've got to go.'

The school hall buzzed with thick, palpable excitement. A queue for entry had begun four hours before the doors opened and, judging by the din of chatter out there, the audience were just as excited as the performers.

'George, Tyler, please stay away from the curtain. We don't want the audience to see you before the opening song—it'll ruin the surprise.' Keeping the kids focused was like trying to herd cats. 'Let's pretend this is the actual competition instead of the fundraiser. Be professional and confident but, most of all, enjoy yourselves. Big smiles.'

'Hey, Miss Sweet. Cute outfit.' There it was again. Behind her. That dark voice that made her weak-kneed. The press of his palm on her back. The scent that made her heart do loop-the-loops. She wasn't sure he'd even turn up after his disappearing act the minute she'd probed a little deeper under that thick skin of his. Even if he didn't have a sign round his neck flashing *keep out*, she'd certainly got the message.

'Nate!' She pulled him to the shadows at the side of the stage, ostensibly to prep him for the show, but in reality to grab a few seconds with him, alone. 'Do you ever approach anyone from the front?'

'And spoil the element of surprise?'

'One of these days you're going to give me a heart attack.' One day? No more days. Two more hours and he'd be gone.

And he looked awful. Sure, he was picture-perfect performance ready, and few would notice the dark shadows round his eyes, the clenched jaw, the hollowed-out cheeks. But she did. She knew enough about Nate Munro to read the signs.

'Big night last night?'

'Yep. And the night before…and the one before that… you get the picture. Too many early mornings and late nights.' How easily he slipped back into his life. At least he hadn't said *too many women*. For that she was grateful. He ran a hand through his masterfully scruffed hair. Which she would not touch. Would. Not. 'Don't worry, I'll live, and I won't let you all down. I'm still match fit.'

'Well, I suppose we should be grateful you're here at all, then, even if you do look like crap.'

'Hey, steady with the compliments—you'll give me a big head.'

'Very unlikely. Is it possible for it to get any bigger?'

'I'll never have a big head with you keeping me grounded.' He grinned, but she couldn't help thinking his deterioration had something to do with their last conversation about Marshall. Clearly there was a lot more to the story than he was prepared to share. But it wasn't her place to ask questions and push him into a corner, she'd learnt to her cost—the last time that had happened he'd screamed at her about breaking trust. And then walked out of her life.

He grinned. 'Excited about tonight?'

'Yes. Very much. Thank you for doing this.'

'My pleasure. To be honest, I wasn't convinced at first, but this whole experience has been...interesting.' His mouth twitched and his arm wrapped round her waist, pressing her long black silk dress to her body as he slipped a nonchalant kiss on her cheek.

The fingers of his other hand played with the way-more-than-she-wanted-to-pay professionally styled curls bouncing around her cheeks. 'And just look at you, sweet thing. Amazing. You've done well for yourself—you should be proud.'

'I am.'

Now his hand ran across the dip of her very bare collarbone sending hot shivers of desire arcing through her.

She reached to the zipper on his leather jacket, and looked up into his face wishing she could stop time and stay wrapped in his arms for a few more minutes.

For for ever? The thought shook through her. Once that had been all she'd dreamed of, but now it seemed a ridiculous idea. Things had changed: *she'd* changed. Moved on, wanted very different things. But it was enough to be the sole focus of those caramel eyes for a few more minutes.

She smiled, warily. 'Listen, I'm sorry about the other night.'

'Hey. Hush.' Pressing a finger to her lips, he stopped her. She remembered the way his mouth had fitted so perfectly over hers, how he had tasted. And her gut twisted with an ache for more.

He shook his head. '*I'm* sorry. It was my fault, not yours. I shouldn't have dodged out so fast, I should have stayed.'

Her heart squeezed. When? Ten years ago? Or the other day?

She laughed it off. 'But that's you all over, Nate. Always rushing on to the next thing.' Always running away when things get tough.

'I like to keep busy—it keeps me out of mischief. I could have done with being busy these last few days.' His eyes widened and she wondered what he'd been doing. But she had no claims on him.

'Please, spare me the gory details.'

'It's not what you think. The only…liaison…I had was with my old mate Jack. *Daniels*. We had some serious catching up to do. He's a good friend, but he does make my head hurt after a while.' As her blood pressure steadied he tipped his head towards the stage. 'They look awesome. You're going to knock that audience's socks off.'

The choir had assembled ready to start, resplendent in their black tuxedoes. 'Gosh yes, I'm so proud of them. They've come so far, and worked so hard. Tonight's just a first step on their journey.'

But for her and Nate it was the end.

'Almost curtain up.' He winked as the front of house dimmed and an expectant hush shivered through the hall. Breathing deeply, he grinned. 'Can you feel that buzz? Man, I love this stuff. Every. Single. Time. It's like a drug. It's what keeps me alive. Break a leg, sweet thing.'

'You too.' She paused, and then words escaped her lips before she had a chance to stop them. 'And then?'

It was almost a whisper, swamped as the music started to play. What she was hoping for she didn't know. A declaration that he felt the same way as she did? Which was unsure and rocky, but turned on. That he wanted to see where these feelings could take them?

She just wanted more time to…to what? To get to know Nathan all over again? No, to understand this new Nate.

The man behind the public image. The one she was already too intrigued by. Mr Wrong.

And not a slipper in sight.

To hell with bloody slippers. A decision crystallised. Every look he gave her told her he wanted her. Even though he would leave. She was okay with that.

She was sick of being scared, allowing her need for control to define her. She would let go. Grasp the passion she'd denied herself for so long. Just once. Give in to dangerous temptation, then she could go back to her nice safe life where passion was a distant memory. Something other people did.

If he asked, she would say yes. She would take him for herself.

The curtain began to open.

He turned to her, his mouth kicked up in a smile that looked a lot like regret. Because, in reality she was way too late. The chances he'd offered her were now just a forgotten living-for-the-moment rock-star whim. He was probably already planning his next conquest.

'And then, Sasha, I'm getting the first plane out of here.'

Once the applause died down Nate took the microphone ready to squeeze the appreciative audience for everything they had. If she wouldn't take a cent from him he'd make sure Sasha got what she needed and more, somehow. It was the least he could do before he headed back home to the States.

'Thanks very much for your support, everyone. Weren't they amazing? There are some buckets going round for your donations—please dig deep. You know it's for a good cause. Let's get this choir to Manchester.'

'Thanks. Wow. That was…bloody brilliant.' Sasha greeted him as he finally left the stage, her smile as bright as the spotlights.

'Language, Miss Sweet. Brilliant? It was epic.' He fist-pumped the air in lieu of picking her up and hugging her. Touching her made him want her even more. He'd almost kissed her backstage, and that would have been a big mistake so close to leaving.

'They were great. They did everything we asked, and more. Man, that was fun.'

'Thank you so much. Just…thank you, thank you. We've made enough money to make Manchester a real trip to remember. It won't matter if we don't win the competition after this—it feels like we've won the jackpot already.' Tiptoeing, she pressed a kiss to his cheek. 'They've excelled under your guidance. You're a natural with kids.'

At the briefest touch of her skin against his heat flared through him; all thought of the choir and the applause faded away. The rush of his usual post-performance heat hit Nate square in the groin, but, instead of being a need for a quick release, this time it was a long intense ache that threatened to overpower him.

The ache belonged to Sasha. Just her. Not the performance. Not the adoration from his fans. Just Sasha. Nothing else matched the adrenaline boost he got just being with her and he didn't want to lose that, not yet.

Her lips parted, just enough for him to see the tip of her tongue, the wet that he wanted to taste. Her breathing quickened and her gaze locked with his. For a nanosecond the air stilled and that invisible connection tightened around them, weaving in more complex patterns, snaring them like a spider's web, until there was nothing, no one in the world but them, caught in a magical sphere from which there was no escape.

The truth flickered in her eyes. She wanted him. And he wanted her. Wanted to kiss that mouth, to explore those curves. To lose himself in her.

But he'd already packed his bags.

'Come with me.' His voice was more growl than groan as he pressed his mouth to her ear. For a second he thought he meant *back to LA*. Anywhere. But he brushed that idea away as too intense, too complex. He couldn't think past now. Here.

Dragging her into the darkest corner he could find, he pressed her against a wall. Ran his fingertips over the curve of her cheek, into her hairline, couldn't take his eyes away from her heated gaze. His thumb ran tiny circles along her jaw until it hit the corner of her mouth, which puckered. But what turned him on most was the sheer need in those eyes.

Before he knew what he was doing he crushed his mouth on hers. This time he didn't want to be gentle, didn't want to savour her taste, he wanted to take her, possess her.

And she responded with equal hunger, a greedy meshing of souls, with a deep thirst for more. Her desire fuelled his as she rocked against him, gentle moans coming from her throat, her hands cupping his backside and pulling him closer until they were body on body, skin on skin.

It was too much, but nowhere near enough.

And all too quickly she pushed away, breathless and hot. 'God, what are we doing?'

Searching her face, he wondered whether she was joking. He couldn't help the smile. 'I think that's pretty obvious.'

'But we can't.'

'We just did.'

'Not here, you noggin. There's…there's too many reasons. There's way too much to do out there. We can't get carried away. Goodness.' She playfully struggled against him, but she was laughing, her head tipped back, and the delicate curve of her throat moved with the musical sound.

He planted a kiss to the racing pulse at her throat, breathed in her scent, and she wrapped her arms around his neck, pressing closer so he could feel the soft shape of her beneath the silky fabric.

'Forget everything else, Sash. Let someone else sort it out. One of the other teachers, the mums. The choir. Somebody. Anybody. But not you.' His hands ran down the back of the soft fabric; on their way they discovered the ridge of a bra strap, the outline of her pants. 'I have plans for you right here.'

'What if the cash gets stolen?'

'You know, you worry too much.'

'Hey, I live in this neighbourhood. I have due cause to worry.' She squirmed as he licked against the nape of her neck, whispering through a stifled giggle, 'Besides, someone might see us.'

'Story of my life.' He sighed and leaned his head against hers. They were hidden enough behind large boxes and electrical equipment, but she had a point.

Sasha always had a good point, but he was always too busy enjoying the moment to think through the consequences of his actions. But, well, he didn't want to let go of *this* moment. 'This thing between us, it isn't going away, is it?'

'No, I guess not.'

'Staying away doesn't help. Being with you makes it worse. D'you think we should do something about it?' When he palmed her breast through the folds of her dress she moaned and pressed harder against him.

'I could be convinced.' She bit her bottom lip and her cheeks pinked. She knew exactly what he was asking, and her blatant answer surprised him. 'But where would we go?'

'I don't know. There's a prowl of photographers out there just waiting to catch me. They'll follow us to my hotel, make a scene.'

Pushing her hands against his chest, she nodded. 'My place, then. They surely won't be interested in me and how I leave this place. My car's out the back. The pink saloon nearest the gym. You want to risk it?'

Good question. Risk what? His privacy? Hers? His heart? 'Do you?'

Stupid to ask her that question—now uncertainty flitted across her face. A sharp intake of breath. A frown. He could see the workings of her mind, the answers she struggled to find. Sasha, who planned everything, who factored danger and risk into every moment. 'I…I don't…know…'

He took one of her hands. 'Sasha, I can't promise you anything, certainly not the stable future you crave. You need to know I am going back to LA.'

So where was he going with this? *Sleep with me. Make love with me. Stay with me, just once.* First time in living memory that he'd had to ask. And he liked her all the more for it.

He hoped she could see that he was being genuine for once in his life, and that this wasn't some kind of play. That it was Sasha he wanted, not just anyone.

Was it? Whether he played her or not, he hoped the end result would be the same. Him. Her. Hot, and sticky.

Her gaze burnt with desire.

He fought the need to have her now against the back wall. But it almost killed him. 'Sasha, I swear to God, if you don't stop looking at me like that I won't be held responsible for the headlines tomorrow. *Teacher and rock star found in flagrante backstage.*'

She ran her finger along his jawline, the passion mingling with anxiety as she struggled with the enticement of living dangerously. Foreign territory for a practical planning kind of girl.

Fiddling with a lock of her hair, she sighed. 'What about your plans? Your flight?'

'It's just an interview. It can wait. I'll reschedule, go tomorrow.' He was losing her.

Kissing her neck seemed to focus her on task—which involved her hand on his back, running up and down his spine. Those lips against his neck. Her breasts pressed tight against him. Her scent stoking the fire burning in his gut. 'What do you say, come on, do something spontaneous, let's have a few more minutes together. I'll make it worth every second, I promise.'

'I don't know…'

'Come on, we're good together—you can't deny that. I'll get Dario to head the press off out the front.'

'So he does have some uses after all. He's starting to grow on me.' Her red curls shivered as she seemed to reconcile some kind of battle going on in her head. She took a long deep breath but didn't come up with the reply he was hedging towards.

'It's an easy answer, woman. Yes or no. No need to make a whole new plan or a quick list of pros and cons. It'll be good, I promise you that.' He spoke into her ear. Slowly. Making sure she understood. 'Very. Very. Good.'

To his relief she nodded. 'Okay, I'll sort out the cash and the mess. Meet you out the back in, what, fifteen minutes?'

'Fifteen? Can't you be any quicker?' Fifteen minutes was enough time for all those doubts to start creeping back. Nuzzling his hardness against her thigh, he nibbled her ear lobe. 'Make it ten?'

Her moan was frank and loud. 'God, if you promise to do that again, I'll be ready in five.'

CHAPTER NINE

SOMEHOW, SASHA COULDN'T remember how, they'd reached her apartment, fallen onto her bed, their kisses hard and hot and turning her brain to mush. Nathan's hands were like magic, sending spasms of ecstasy through her with every touch. She wanted more of his kisses. She wanted him naked. She wanted him now.

She fumbled with his belt, tugged at his zip, the hardness of his erection making her stomach clench in anticipation. And just a little fear. He was so big. So hard.

You can handle this.

He lay against her, eyes dark with frank desire as he unfastened her bra and cupped her breast. 'Hey, slow down, Sasha. We've got all night.' His head tipped and he sucked her nipple into his mouth, sending heat shimmering through to her core. 'You're right, you have changed. You're in a hurry.'

She wanted to tell him, no. That she was still the same scared person underneath, that she didn't know if she would be enough for him, that she didn't know what she was doing, but, God, it felt so good.

He pressed against her, the thick weight of him, the smell of him filling her body with sensations she'd never had before, breathtaking, heart-stalling sensations that made her lose touch with reality. Her hands ran along the waistband of his trousers to the hard-muscled V of his abdomen as she relished his sharp intake of breath, his skin puckering under her fingers; his T-shirt, like her dress, long since cast aside, who knew where. 'Sorry. I just…I just…'

She needed to have him before her courage faltered.

He stopped her shaking hand with his. 'I know. Crazy, eh? But take it steady. I've waited a long time for this and now I want to enjoy you.' His tongue ran tiny circles down her ribcage, across her abdomen, tracing a wet trail towards her pants, his hands making her sigh with pleasure as he stroked the inside of her thigh. 'I want to make you moan.'

She did, long and hard. And again as he ripped her pants aside, opened her legs and slid his fingers over her opening. Fierce heat almost engulfed her. 'Oh, God. Oh, God. Oh—'

As she writhed against his hand a delicious ache deep inside began to swell, flushing her body in heat, a feeling she was losing herself to something beautiful, amazing. She needed more pressure, more heat…Losing herself. Losing…

Stop.

No.

Clear as day, the words rang loudly in her head. *Stop. Stop.*

No!

She clutched the duvet in her fist. Shifted away from his hand.

Why? Why always this? Why couldn't it be different with Nathan? She *wanted* to submit to the pleasure he gave her. She *wanted* to be carried away on a tide of passion. She *wanted* to lose control.

But it was as if she were outside her body looking down on them on the bed, all feelings bolted in a flurry of panic. The surge from his touch cut, like a power outage.

He followed her up the bed, his hands still locked on her buttocks. 'You okay?'

'I…um…'

In the dim light she watched confusion flit across his face. *Yeah, you and me too.* He shifted next to her and stroked a knuckle down her cheek. 'Did I tell you how beautiful you are?'

She nodded, curling into his hand, caught her bottom lip with her teeth. 'Yes.'

'Do you believe me?' He thought she was worried about how she looked? Just like all the other Hollywood women he usually slept with, no doubt. If only it were that simple. 'You're so...real, Sash. Raw. Honest. The most beautiful woman I've ever met.'

Bringing her face to his, he dropped feather kisses along her swollen mouth, to her neck. Her eyes fluttered closed as she tried to relax into his arms again.

But she couldn't. After a moment of trying she put her hands on his shoulders and gave gentle pressure. 'I'm sorry. I'm not ready for this.'

He smiled so tenderly it almost took her breath away. 'What is it? What's wrong?' Then he hit his head with his palm, eyes wide. Was he covering up a *laugh*? 'Tell me you're not still a virgin? Surely...'

'No.' But she might as well be. A rash of heat bloomed in her core and spread out to her skin. How to say this? 'I mean...there have been a couple of times. I never really... well, it didn't do much for me.'

'Seriously, girl. You've been doing it with the wrong men.'

As if she didn't know that already.

But it wasn't really their fault. She'd been too wound up, too worried about whether she could do it, about giving herself up to someone else, each thrust had caused her pain and the more she'd tensed, the worse it had become. Until she'd given up trying.

'It hurts, usually. I can't ever seem to relax properly. And I've never...you know...come.'

His laugh was soft. 'But I think you almost did.'

'That's the point exactly. *Almost.*'

'You just need to go with the flow. Let yourself ride with it. Let go.'

'Easy for you to say. You're so laid-back you're hardly holding on in the first place.' She wanted to hide her face in embarrassment. This was what she was, after twenty-seven years? She'd managed easy relationships with the kids at school and her friends, family—sure. She'd never given any more of herself than she needed, always kept something back. Intimacy scared her but not as much as trusting someone.

And with Nathan? The thought of giving herself over to someone so sexually experienced, and who instilled such fierce emotions in her, was terrifying.

No. Impossible.

And now he would leave and she was a big fat failure.

But instead of leaving he covered her with the duvet and spooned against her, his chest against her back. For a moment she thought he was going to try to sleep, as with two fingers he closed both her eyelids. He spoke in a soft voice as he cuddled against her. 'It's okay. Let's take it really slow. Tell me, what do you want, Sasha? What do you like?'

'I don't know. What do you mean?' She tried to sit up but he held her close.

'Hey, it's just talking. That's all. You can do that.' He chuckled. 'I don't want a checklist. I want you to tell me what turns you on. Close your eyes. Do you like it when I kiss you?'

'Of course.' She closed her eyes again, sank into the pillows and thought about his kisses. They made her feel hot. So hot. Wanted. Sexy. 'Yes.'

'Tell me, then. Say it.'

'I like it when you kiss me.'

'Do you like my tongue in your mouth?'

'Yes.' She swallowed, hard. Her mouth suddenly dry and wet at the same time.

'Tell me more. Do you like it when I kiss your nipples?'

'Yes.' God, yes. 'But I'm no good at this.'

'It's not a test. Just say it. I like it when you kiss my nipples.'

'I like it when you kiss…' She hardly recognised her own voice; it was thick and hoarse.

'Kiss what?'

'My nipples.' Her breasts ached and tingled for his hands, his mouth. All air seemed to have been sucked out of her lungs; she focused on breathing. In. Out.

She felt a gentle pressure against her hips as he began to rock against her. Just a little, but it sent skittering electricity through her. She pressed back against him, feeling his erection on her bottom. Wanting to touch it.

But he held her hand, kissed the soft underside of her wrist, leant his head against hers, whispering into her ear, 'What else do you like, Sasha? Did you like it when I touched you?'

'Oh. God. Yes.' Was it the sensation of his breath against her neck, or just thinking about his hands on her that made her shiver with anticipation?

'I know you did. I liked it too.' But he didn't lower his head to her thighs as she thought he might. Hoped he might.

His fingers tiptoed to her outer thigh. Then her inner thigh. Stroking slowly. So slowly she thought she might explode if he didn't touch her. There. Her whole body screamed out for his touch. 'Yes. There. Please, Nate. There.'

'Not yet. Just wait.' He rocked. She rocked back against his thickness. If she shifted her leg…oh. She felt him pressing along the edge of her sex. A fug of desire filled her head.

'What else do you like, Sasha?' Then his thumb found

the spot. Sweet soft pressure that wasn't nearly enough to satisfy her.

'I want…I want you to…' She couldn't think past his thumb circling and pressing, past the wild hunger swirling through her body. Through her head. She was losing herself.

'What do you want?'

Losing…

'What do you want?' His voice was louder now, focusing her on him. 'Sasha. Tell me what you want.'

'I want this.' Fierce need swelled up once again from deep inside, in a huge crescendo that she rode. Wave after wave of delicious peaks, each time bigger, better than the last. But still not enough…'I want this. I want…' Harder. Faster. Deeper. 'Oh, God. Oh, God. I want you.'

Her fingers slipped round his erection and she turned to face him, steering him towards her, her breath coming in short gasps. Nate didn't know if he could hold on long enough to get the condom on. If she could hold on. She was so close to the edge.

'Now, Nathan, please.'

'I don't want to hurt you. Steady, wait.'

'Now. *Please.*'

He quickly sheathed himself and pushed gently into her. Felt the stretch, the hesitation, the shock, but he kept up the pressure with his fingers, stroking and rubbing, until she relaxed. As she bucked against his hand he eased deeper into her heat.

For the first time ever he needed solid self-control. Didn't know if he could dredge it up. He had to get this right. For her. For himself. He had to show her what she'd been missing out on for so long. But watching her finally so close to the edge, unbuttoning that prim uptight exterior, feeling her nails rake against his back, had him alight with a raging fire.

Tight. Hot. Wet.

Slowly at first, until he couldn't hold back any more. He wanted to bury himself so deep inside her, deeper and deeper still.

And she met him stroke for stroke. Her legs inching up his thighs as she gripped and bucked against him. He found her mouth and kissed her greedily, taking every ounce of her that he could. She arched, her head thrown back, her gaze catching his, consuming him.

Until…

Until he thought he might lose himself completely in an arc of blinding pleasure, in the soft sound of her cries, in her sweet tightness as she finally let herself go and took him with her.

Twisting out of the tumble of sheets Sasha jolted upright and looked around her bedroom, then down at her bed.

Oh, double merry hell. It hadn't been a dream at all. A three-times-a-night kind of dream. A Best. Sex. Ever. Dream.

Next to her Nathan slept, his hair messed up, little laughter lines around his eyes. Butt naked, the cotton sheet strategically covering one of his best features, he looked like a model in a magazine shoot.

In her bed!

Her heart stuttered just to look at him. Even though she'd tried hard to prevent it she knew she was losing herself to him, little by little.

She hadn't known it was possible to soar so high, or how amazing sex could be when she finally let herself relax into it. To feel like a real woman. To feel wanted by a man like Nate. She'd grasped at an opportunity instead of planning the pros and cons. And there'd been a whole lot of pros.

But what on earth happened now? She hadn't planned for that either. Hadn't planned for the completeness of having him inside her and the emptiness of knowing he was going to leave. Or the stark fact that it was very unlikely that slipper-man, should he ever bother to rock on up, would be able to make her feel that absolute glow that Nathan had made her feel last night.

Torn between needing him gone so she could clear her head, and wanting to snuggle down next to him, she pulled on a robe and wandered through to the lounge, looking for some middle ground.

Facts were:

1) He lived in LA. She lived here.

2) His life involved chaos and extremes. She liked order.

3) He was a moment-by-moment type of guy. She planned everything to the nth degree.

Until last night, when she'd decided to be someone different.

But he wasn't her kind of man.

Which brought her to undeniable fact number four: he was unpredictable, volatile and untamed. Everything she hated; everything she avoided in a relationship.

And no amount of backward planning would extricate her from the world-shifting uncertainty hammering in her chest.

'Sasha?' His sleep-filled voice made her jump and ramped up the jittery butterflies dancing in her stomach. 'It's only six-thirty—the day hasn't started yet. What's going on?'

Every cell in her body craved his touch, heat surged through her veins, but she busied herself in the kitchenette, not knowing the rules for this kind of thing. But she bet it wasn't making a scene. She found him a smile. 'There you are again with the behind thing.'

'Sasha, this postage-stamp-sized apartment leaves little room for the element of surprise. I could probably have poked my head out of bed and you'd have seen me from here.' He leaned against the kitchen bench, half-zipped jeans slung on his hips—there was no way he could be wearing any underwear with them riding so low.

The thought of him commando, of what was under that denim, had her mouth watering and her body prickling with heat. The hard wall of his chest rippled as he moved. She remembered the feel of it under her fingertips, the slick press of it against her naked body.

The butterflies fluttered against her heart, sending ripples of a strange kind of pain in her chest.

She tucked her confusion away and quieted the darned insects. 'Don't you have a plane to catch, Nate? Somewhere to be?'

'You want to get rid of me already?' Was that a flicker of relief in his eyes? Did he feel as confused as she did? He took the mug of coffee she offered him. 'No problem. I've rearranged my flight for one o'clock this afternoon.'

Probably the first flight out, so he couldn't wait to leave. 'I see, and is everyone okay with that?' Was she okay with that?

He blinked. 'I'm the star, Sasha. I get to decide what happens.'

What the—? Back to business as usual, then. The tender amazing lover had done a bunk, replaced by the egomaniac. 'Er...not with me, you don't. I make my own decisions—at least, I'm used to negotiating, talking...'

'Someone's tetchy this morning. Not enough sleep perhaps?' He gave her a half-smile that told her he was struggling with the realities of spur-of-the-moment sex too. Or maybe it was just a reaction to her mood, which she knew was off. But she needed to protect herself somehow.

In lieu of there being nowhere else for him to sit he joined her on the sofa. 'I mean, I get to organise my timetable. If that doesn't work for you then I can change it. Push it back, bring it forward.'

'Forward might be a good idea. The world goes on regardless.'

He looked at her for a long moment. 'Regardless of what?'

'This. Last night.'

'Look, Sash, I had a great time, the best. Really, the best.' He hesitantly took her hand. 'But I do have to go. I know this is hard.'

'It's fine.' She shook her hand free from his, reluctant to open herself up to even more emotional exposure. The more locked-off she made herself, the better.

'No, it isn't fine at all. I can see it all over your face. You did something amazing—and, Sasha, we were good. So, so good. But...' he smoothed her hair with his palm '...I can't give you anything more. I was always upfront about that.'

Tears pricked at the backs of her eyes but she steadfastly would not let him see them. She'd known this all along and it was only her stupid heart doing a little rebellion.

She added lightness to a voice that was anything but. 'Hey, I'm not the clingy type so don't worry, I won't accost you at art-gallery parties or be rude to other women you're with. You have your life, I have mine and this was just a bit of random fun.'

So why weren't they laughing?

After taking another gulp of coffee he dipped his gaze and seemed lost in thought. Or a struggle. Or something. But when he looked back to her his eyes were softer, his smile almost tender. 'Maybe I could come back again. Some time.'

'Sure. In another ten years?' *Damn.* The words just blurted out. It wasn't as if she'd waited for him to come back; she'd got on with her life despite him leaving. *Hell.*

The sound of a heavy-duty motorbike engine revving and growling down in the street made them both jump.

'Honestly, some people, it's way too early for that.' She turned towards the noise, which set her nerves on edge. Unease shuddered down her spine as she watched Nathan storm to the window, the chill in the room taking a further nosedive.

But the growl didn't stop, accompanied now by a darker, more sinister one from Nathan's throat that sent her heart racing and a sickening drop in her stomach. He peered through a chink in the closed curtains, a shaft of bright early sunshine illuminating his straight back and hands fisting at his sides. 'What the—? Scumbags.'

His voice was too loud and too angry as he dropped the curtain but Nate couldn't contain his anger, not even for Sasha. Not even after the best night of his life. Her smell coated his skin, his hair. The taste of her lingered in his mouth. And his body ached to take her straight back to bed for a rerun. But that wasn't going to happen—she'd made that clear. And she was right.

He didn't do this—staying over. Wanting more.

So he didn't know whether his inflated reaction was caused by the guys outside, or the fact he'd been thrown off kilter by the mixed-up feelings swirling round his chest. Factor in a mess of photographers and his mood was shot. 'They must have followed us last night when I thought we'd given them the slip.'

'Who? What is it? What's happening?' Instead of coming to the window she shunted further into the sofa cushions, eyes wide and spooked.

And that was the moment he determined she couldn't be part of his life long-term. Jasmine, Cara, the plastic sisterhood—they all adored publicity and fed off it like piranhas.

Sasha wasn't like them. She was a regular—no, a stellar—high-school teacher who wanted to stay being just that.

She didn't crave fame for her own end. And he'd dragged her into a chaos of his own making. He should have kept away. Should have gone back to his hotel alone last night, instead of giving in to temptation.

But she'd been so sweet to put her inexperience in his hands, then so incredibly hot, it wasn't something he'd ever regret. Perfect. Bloody perfect. He just needed to get his head round it, but that didn't seem to be happening.

'Cameras, paps...lowlife.' He forced his voice to soften. 'They either followed us, or had a tip-off and spent the night trawling the Internet to find things out about you.'

'Pull the curtains closed, then. I don't want them here. How can we get rid of them?'

'Without making a scene? Very little. But they'll know now what you do as a job. What your credit rating is. What kind of junk...er car you drive.'

'If you're trying to make me feel better, it's not working.' An indignant smile broke through the frown. 'I happen to love that car. I bought it when I was twenty-two, the down-payment was from my first pay packet.'

'Boy, you teachers must have really low wages.'

Perfectly shaped eyebrows peaked. 'Yeah. Ha. Ha. It's reliable—mostly. And it's pink, easy to spot in a car park. Bonus.'

'It's a wreck and clearly way too distinctive to be a get-away car. Let me buy you another one? Whatever you want, it's the least I can do.'

Sitting up, she frowned. 'What? You sleep with me and then want to pay me out with a car? What is this? Guilt money or...worse? I don't want anything from you. That's not what this is about.'

'Hey. Stop right there.' Whatever else happened here he needed to erase that hurt simmering in her eyes. No way did he want that to be the last image he had of her. 'Most people do want something from me. I just can't get used to the fact that you don't.' But he wouldn't put up with that kind of accusation.

He tipped her chin up so he could see her face properly. So she could see his. 'I slept with you because you're beautiful and hot, and I like you. And I'm glad I did.' And of all the women he'd slept with, none had made him feel so stirred up that he didn't know how to leave. Or how to stay.

'Oh. Okay. Me too…I suppose.' She managed a weak smile and looked up at him under thick black eyelashes.

It took a huge amount of effort not to say something stupid or sentimental that would cause more damage in the long run. 'And I want to buy you a car because I can afford to. That's all. That car is so old it could be dangerous.' He flicked his thumb to the window. 'Like these idiots here are dangerous. They can ruin lives.'

'Yes, I know all about that too. Thank you very much.' She shook her head as if closing off that line of thought. She was good at that—bringing down the barriers about her private past or about any kind of emotional pain. 'How can we get rid of them? Police?'

'Unlikely. They've never been much help before. A lot of them think celebs are fair game, as far as I can see.' But Sasha wasn't.

Anger swelled from nowhere and before he could contain it his fist landed on the coffee table with a thump.

Her shoulders twitched and the spooky look on her face darkened. 'Hey. Stop that. Go ruin your own stuff. Leave mine alone.'

And he was making things worse, again, in his bid to protect her. Where did that come from?

Feisty she might be, but there she sat in the tiniest lounge in living history, lush red hair corkscrewing around her shoulders, completely oblivious to the freak show she was now part of. Every part of her life would be scrutinised and picked apart. There was nothing for it but to shelter her from it all.

But how?

He should just take her lead and leave her to it.

But…well, he couldn't let the circling sharks have their feed on her, not when it was his fault they were here in the first place.

Kneeling down at the sofa, he tugged her hand. 'Come to the bedroom and start packing some clothes while I make a few calls. You need to get away for a few days until all this interest has died down. You're not at school on Monday?'

She tugged her hand back. 'No. We have Spring Bank Holiday week…but I need to work, refine the choreography.'

'Excellent. I'll get onto it. You don't need to be here. You can work on routines wherever you are.'

'Please, it's not necessary. I can look after myself.'

The trill of her cellphone distracted her. 'Hello? Yes, this is Sasha…What? No! No. Go away. Go to hell.'

'What was that about?' Just seeing the panic in her eyes made his gut clench.

'It's just some jerk wanting to know how many times we had sex last night. Did I want an exclusive?' She rolled her eyes. 'Who cares about these things?'

'You don't know these people and the lengths they will go to. We need to lay low for a few days or there'll be lots more calls like that. And if they don't get a story they'll delve into your past, or worse, make something up. Print lies.'

Horrified, she held her head in her hands. 'I couldn't bear that. My sisters would cope—Cassie would probably love the attention—but Mum doesn't deserve to have her past trawled through the papers, not all that stuff about my dad. It was bad enough at the time. She's finally managed to put it all behind her.'

His hands were on her shoulders now, closer than he should be, but he just couldn't help himself. 'So you need to pack.'

'Wait…I know. I know. I just need some time. To think. To organise…'

'Sasha, the sooner we get out—'

'I know. I'm just thinking…'

If he'd had more time and less sense he'd have crushed those lips with his mouth, taken her to bed and kissed her back to some kind of better mood. But instead he picked her up, threw her over his shoulder ignoring her protestations and squeals, and carried her into the cupboard she had the audacity to call a bedroom.

Dumping her on the unmade bed that was still warm from their bodies, he stood over her, refusing to take any more nonsense. Someone had to take control here, and it wasn't going to be her. 'Okay. Take ten seconds to think it over, write a list or a spreadsheet or whatever you need to do to get your head round it all. Ten. That's all you have. Then I'm phoning my pilot.'

Still shocked at the fireman's lift, she stared at him as if trying to process the turn of events. Her shoulders slumped forward, her expression turning from confused to blatant flustered.

Man, it was downright dangerous when she flustered. Her pretty nose crinkled, her cheeks blazed and her eyes got a panicky mist that made him want to wrap her up in his arms. 'Nate, I can't just go somewhere on the cuff like this. I just can't.'

'Yes, you can.' Her clothes were so neatly stacked he had no trouble finding what she might need. 'I'll fly you somewhere safe.'

'Fly? I don't need to go that far away. I can manage fine. I'll drive.'

He pointed to the street outside from where excited chatter permeated their privacy. 'Sasha, they'll chase you from one end of this country to another. If we fly out somewhere then we can muddy the flight details a little. Throw them off scent.'

We? We? He was going to go back to LA and send her to a nice private spa in Switzerland or France—on her own.

You. Not *we.* Goddamn.

'Together?'

Shoot. He exhaled good and hard. Spending more time with her was the far side of crazy, but it made a lot of sense. He could lockdown the house, monitor the papers, keep her safe. Rerun last night…

'This is my fault, I should…look after you. Just for a few days…a week at most.' It was a step closer to protecting her than letting her stay somewhere, spooked, on her own. 'And I need to do it right this time.'

'This time? This time? I don't understand. You never needed to look after me before.' Her eyes grew wider. 'Hang on…this isn't just about me and the paparazzi, is it?'

He'd hoped that little slip had gone under the radar too. But no. Nothing went under the radar with Sasha. How was she so perceptive? Feigning nonchalance, he shrugged and struggled for words. Was fluster contagious? 'No…look, I don't know. Leave it alone.'

'It's about something else too. Someone else.' She clicked her fingers as she thought, a wave of a frown on her forehead. 'Of course…it's about Marshall. Something about protecting him? Or failing to. Am I right?'

Yeah? Then she'd just worked out something he hadn't even known about himself. Maybe she was right, maybe everything came back to how he'd let his brother down.

But somehow he doubted it—he'd got over that years ago. Hadn't he?

A sharp ache tore through his chest at the thought of Marshall's smiling face. He buried the pain back. No time for that now. Or ever. 'Hurry and pack. We haven't got time to talk about this.'

'Yes, we do.' With a determined twinkle in her eye she sat on the edge of the bed and folded her arms. 'I can wait, just like those guys outside. As long as it takes, Mr Hotshot. So you can either tell me what this is all about, or you can sit here with me for who knows how long? Because I'm not heading off on any jaunt without knowing the real reason you need to save me.'

Oh, she was good. Holding *him* hostage when he was trying to protect her. But he never shared this.

Never.

Sasha watched, stunned, as he stuffed her clothes into a holdall he'd grabbed from under her bed, doing everything he could to avoid eye contact. 'Nathan. Talk.'

He looked up and opened his mouth, apparently shocked into speaking. 'Marshall had a hard time at school. It was my fault. I pushed for him to go there.' He stopped stuffing. 'Sorry? Why do you need to hear this. Now?'

'Because I do. And you need to tell me, or we don't go anywhere. Whatever the cost. It was challenging for him, sure, a lot of special-needs kids find mainstream school hard. But you did what you thought was best for him.'

He laughed, but it was hollow and cold. 'Like I knew? I *believed* he should go to a regular school instead of living with a label. I *believed* only I knew what was the right thing for him. So I forced the school to take him, in the only way I knew how.'

After his father went to prison Nate had been a gangly teenager forced into taking control of a situation he just didn't know how to deal with. But that had never deterred him.

'I was the man of the house, but I didn't know crap about being a man, other than shouting loudly and getting my own way with violence. So I just walked into the school office and insisted they take him, even accusing them of discriminating against him. They didn't like that.'

'I imagine they didn't. But Marshall loved the school, right? It was definitely the best decision for him.' She reached across the duvet and tried to pull him to sit opposite her. But he resisted.

Instead, he stared into a spot just past her shoulder. 'At first he did, but gradually he grew quieter and less willing to join in things. The only place he seemed happy was the choir. Eventually he admitted he was being bullied.'

'Oh, Nate. That's awful. I had no idea.'

Nate smoothed a palm over the back of his neck. 'I thought he'd brush the whole thing off—he'd always known he was different and accepted it. But then one day I found him in tears holding a note from one of his classmates. It said he should never have been born, that he was dirty and no one liked him. Seemed he'd been bullied for a while.'

'That's terrible. You should have told someone—a teacher. The headmaster.'

'I dealt with it. It didn't need making public. I was the big brother—it was my job to sort it out.' He shrugged nonchalantly, his voice steady and detached, as he slipped back behind the public mask he wore. 'At least that was the plan. I was pretty sure no one would listen anyway. I was having a bad day already and this made it a whole lot worse. I saw red. Stormed out and hunted down the culprit, some no-hoper called Craig. He and I had a brief exchange of words and then—'

'Then you hit him,' she interrupted, the events of their last night together now clear. The way he'd turned up at her house, dishevelled, animated. She'd initially thought his rocky emotional state had been to do with an argument they'd had about her refusal to talk to him about her past. How she didn't trust him enough. He'd been so passionate. Ardent.

And that passion had stirred something so deep in her, as it did again now, they'd finally almost made love, so close.

But then the authorities had hammered her door down in search of him. 'Your knuckles, I remember, they were sore and swollen, but you never did give me the full story, clearly.'

'Because you did exactly what everyone else did. You looked at me as if you'd been expecting it all along. That I was no different from my useless violent father.'

Was that how he saw it? Pain settled under her ribcage. 'No. I knew you were different from him. I knew everyone saw a different side from the one I saw.'

'Sasha, the look in your eyes stayed with me for longer than I cared to remember.'

Because the whole sordid scenario had revived the memories of the night her father had died. Police at the door, shouting. Things getting way out of control. She couldn't witness that kind of aggression and violence again, no matter how justified. And not from someone she'd loved. Or at least, believed she did.

But he'd been acting out of pure love, trying to protect his brother. He'd chosen her as the only person he could turn to when he needed comfort. For love? Trust?

So she could see now how her betrayal, along with the way the town turned their backs on him, had forced him to leave and then spend the next few years forging emotional detachment. The drinking, the endless string of women, the wild parties. And, by saving herself, she'd been partly to blame for that. No wonder the man screamed non-commitment—he probably believed everyone he ever loved would let him down. Walk away. Turn away.

Small wonder then, the rage, the hot-headedness, the ill-contained anger that stirred something raw and new in her, that both attracted and troubled her.

She wanted to pull him back down on the bed and make him understand that she'd had other reasons to walk away all those years ago. But with his tensed muscles and the mask of impartiality he'd slipped back on she didn't think he'd allow it. 'If you'd only explained, I'd have listened.'

'No, you wouldn't. You shut down. And I wasn't making a lot of sense. I'd completely lost control. They had to drag me off Craig. I was an animal. Worse. The only reason they didn't press charges was because I had the letter evidence that Craig had been bullying Marshall.'

'But even so, you can't blame yourself for what happened.'

'Can't I? I failed Marshall by putting him in that situation. I might as well have bullied him myself. I did the wrong thing to get him out of it. Craig ended up in Intensive Care and Marshall never really recovered. He died a couple of years later.'

'I'm so, so sorry.'

'Yes. Well, it was a long time ago.' And with that he turned, swung the wardrobe door open with a crash and reached for more of her clothes.

Conversation over. He'd reached his limit; that was clear.

It almost broke her heart to see him so closed-off, particularly when it was partly her fault. But he was the kind of guy who would take responsibility square on his shoulders, and would never back down.

She didn't know a way forward and didn't want to fill the space with the sound of her own voice so she gathered her toiletries from the bathroom, imagining what the next

few days with him would be like when there was so much
between them.

An intense connection. Sizzling but bruised. Ice and
heat.

Either way, if she didn't protect herself, she was going
to get burnt.

Five minutes later he zipped the holdall and pulled out
his phone. The smile he gave her was muted, as if a whirl-
wind of emotion had rattled through and he was dealing
with the aftermath. He stretched out a hand and when she
took it in hers it was warm and large and solid. Just like
his heart—if only he'd let himself believe it.

She smiled back at him.

Then before she could register it his lips were on hers, a
sublime pressure that reverberated through her body, melting her bones, leaving her craving more. And more. And…

She kissed him back, hard and deep, gripping his shoulders, forgetting the tension and the uncertainty, the hurt
of the past. When he pulled her to him she fitted perfectly
into his arms and let the fire raging inside her smoulder
and burn some more. The heat subsumed her until she was
lost in him, in this, and she wasn't sure she even wanted
to find a way back.

Eventually he pulled away, his rough edges softened
slightly and, in his face, she caught a glimpse of the man
who'd made love to her last night. His voice was thick and
hoarse. 'Ready?'

For more of that? Hell, yes, even though she hadn't got
any kind of plan as to how she'd survive the next few days
in one piece. 'So where will we go?'

'Ah, God, I don't know, Sasha. How does Italy sound?'

CHAPTER TEN

'I DON'T SUPPOSE you'd consider putting the guidebook down and actually taking in the amazing Florence scenery?'

Nathan's teasing was fair, Sasha decided. His mood had lightened with every mile they'd travelled away from Chesterton, but flashes of it lingered in his taut stance as he looked at her with a half-bemused frown.

He'd brought her to the one place in the whole world she wanted to visit, had even organised an unprecedented private half-hour to view the most iconic landmark in the city. So he was right—she should be paying attention.

She looked out from the top of the startling black and white marble Duomo across sun-drenched butterscotch buildings topped with terracotta roofs.

The view from the plane had shown her a patchwork of piazzas, the magical river Arno, and lush green Tuscan hills that protected the city. But nothing compared to breathing real Florence air and seeing the architecture close-up.

At every turn there was an ancient cathedral, a church, an ornate building. Florence oozed charm and history, complete with delicious smells that made her stomach grumble: rich garlic, pungent rosemary and dark thick coffee.

She hit him on the shoulder with the book. 'I'm just reading up about the place. This book suggests the top ten things to do in Tuscany. I want to tick them all off. Did you know you can hire segways to ride around the piazzas, or take a horse and carriage to explore the old quarters?'

'No, Sasha, I didn't.'

'Or that legend says Florence is so breathtakingly beautiful it can make you swoon with its utter majesty?'

He stared out over the rooftops, hands deep in his pockets, and breathed out hard. 'No, Sasha, I didn't.'

'Did you—?'

'Here, give me that…' Snatching the book from her hand, he scanned the list, snapped the book closed and shoved it into a nearby litterbin. 'That's enough of that.'

Tension squeezed her stomach as she looked from his hand to the bin. 'But…'

He held her gaze, the tautness of his jaw and the coolness in his eyes putting her on edge.

If this was how it was going to be she didn't want to stay another minute. 'Clearly you don't want to be here, Nate. I'm sorry if you came under duress. You can always leave. For that matter, so can I.'

'I'm sorry. I'm just a little on edge.' He ran a hand over the back of his neck and looked at her with the same kind of confusion she was feeling.

'Yes, well, this is all weird for me too. I didn't exactly plan it.'

He laughed, just. 'No, Sasha. No, you didn't. And I don't want to be constricted by someone else's idea of how to have a good time. I think I can work that out all by myself. That's a rubbish list, for a start.' Warmth returned to his eyes and he began to smile. Slowly at first. Until his features softened along with his stance. 'It's nothing like *my* top ten things to do in Tuscany.'

'That's because your top ten things are probably X-rated.'

His eyes glinted, giving her every indication that while they were here he had definite plans of his own. 'There's nothing wrong with that. This is a kind of holiday after all. And when you're on holiday you're meant to do things you enjoy. Not things people tell you to do.'

A holiday. A break. A fling. *Strictly temporary.* A fantasy that wasn't even hers—she'd just borrowed it until Mr Boring But Safe came driving along in his racing-green family-sized saloon. A fantasy that clearly involved more time in bed if she wanted it.

All she had to do was agree.

It had taken only a matter of days to swerve her from her life plan. And now, here she was with the poster boy for effortless seduction, on the run from the press. She couldn't have made it up. And she sure as heck hadn't put up much of a fight. One whiff of him opening up to her and she'd been putty in those exquisitely toned arms.

But God, the way he made her feel with just one glance from those intense whisky eyes and the mesmerising just-for-her smile he was flashing at her now… Some of her misgivings began to drift away with the gentle Tuscan breeze.

His fingers stole up her back. 'And seeing as you're getting so good at it…'

'That's because I have a very good teacher.' The giggle that came from her throat surprised her, she never giggled. Well, heck, it seemed she did now. She was changing in surprising ways.

'Takes one to know one.' He shrugged. 'But we do have a lot more to cover…'

He'd put himself out for her—the least she could do was enjoy it. She could do this. She could enjoy him and this fantasy while still protecting herself. She could. All she had to do was let go. It would seem very rude not to.

And fit in as much sightseeing as humanly possible. 'But please can we visit the Ponte Vecchio, the Uffizi…?'

'I've arranged a private viewing at the Uffizi at three.

Before that we can take a drive to the bridge. There's an amazing gelato shop just the other side.'

'Okay.' She turned to take the rickety worn steps back down to ground level. 'So, bridge, then ice cream, then Uffizi? What about—?'

'Sasha, your lists are starting to drive me crazy.' He shook his head. 'I need something to distract me. Luckily, I know just the thing...'

He pushed her against the old cool wall, imprinted no doubt with hundreds of years of stolen moments just like this.

The moment his mouth found hers she forgot the buildings and the art and the book in the bin; the only thing she wanted to look at was his face as he kissed her. To commit this moment to memory so she could bring it out when she was old and grey and remember it. Remember him.

The kiss was soft and gentle, not the heated urgent need of desperation and fire. The kind of kiss you sank into and never wanted to be rescued from. If she hadn't been leaning against the wall she'd have fallen, her legs woozy with pleasure and the swell in her heart.

'And after the sightseeing...' She gave him her best seductive smile. 'What will we do then?'

'You want another list? Yes, I suppose you do.' He nuzzled against the dip of her neck, his hand cupping her breast making every cell in her body scream for skin on skin. 'Okay, my house, my list. Let me see...lazy mornings in my four-poster at the castello...long, long nights...You get the picture.'

'Typical man. Sex...and sex.'

'You have a problem with that?'

She twisted to face him, giving him what she knew was a full-watt smile, wishing...wishing what? That he'd said he wanted something more than physical? 'But you can do that anywhere.'

'Is that an offer? You want to start now? Only, I think the priests downstairs might have a problem with that...'

'Oh, yes. Good point. Save it for later.'

He groaned. 'I can't wait.'

'But you have to wait...' Her fingers trailed towards his jeans zipper, and she heard his gasp, the increase in his breathing. 'Just for the record, Nathan, your lists are getting better all the time.'

She swallowed deeply, relishing her new-found sexual power—instilling such desire in a man, making him want more. Making him want *her*. If only she could have the same effect on his brain and find out what was really going on in that superstar fame-filled head of his.

He gave her so much...but never everything...allowing her a glimpse of his inner private self, before slamming the shutters down pretty resolutely. She knew he was damaged but a survivor, tender and funny. Reluctantly kind. Sexy as anything. She knew exactly what he wanted her to know—and no more.

Strip away the rest of that alpha bravado and what else would she find underneath? Did she really want to know?

Three days, and a lot of extra-curricular activity later, Nate sat in a private dining room overlooking his local town's busy piazza. Strains of soft music floated through the shutters as the local community began their evening promenade, smiling, nodding and taking absolutely no notice of Nate and his beautiful dinner guest. For that, he was grateful.

'*Risotto ai funghi, per favore?*' Sasha smiled up at the waiter, nibbling her bottom lip as if worried about her accent.

Nate's stomach clenched. First smile of the day and she'd given it to someone else.

He leaned across the table. 'If I'd known you spoke the

language I'd have let you do the talking instead of my pathetic efforts.'

'I've only just plucked up enough courage to try it out. When in Rome, and all that… I've got one of those language DVDs at home.' She smiled for him, just. 'Goes to show how little you really know about me.'

'I know the best bits very well. But I'm always open to a reminder.'

His gaze travelled down her body, lingered over flawless breasts that he ached to touch again and again.

Her eyes widened, and even though she was pretending to be shocked he caught the spark and fire and heard the crackle of desire in her throat as she spoke. 'Nathan! Please don't look at me like that.'

'Like what?'

'Like you want to eat me.'

'But I do.' Seemed he'd lost his appetite for anything else lately. This time her smile was genuine, as was the full-body blush.

'And what about your *Bistecca alla Fiorentina*?'

'Oh, the food can wait.' He slipped into the seat next to her, unable to wait any longer to feel the brush of her skin against his. Cupping her cheek, he turned her to face him. By God, he'd go to hell for this. 'But this can't.'

He ran his tongue along her bottom lip, felt her brief hesitation, then his heart lifted as she opened her mouth, a tiny growl deep in her throat. He held her face in his hands. 'I want you. Here,' he groaned.

She shifted away from him. 'The food will be here in a minute. We can't keep doing this. We're going to get banned from every eatery in Greve.'

He looked across the candlelit empty room towards the closed door. Knew the waiters would keep their distance unless absolutely necessary. 'We could…if we wanted to. I want to.'

'I can tell. But I'm an upstanding citizen, not a rock star with no morals.'

Something was bugging her and he had no idea what.

Worse—he cared. Cared that she was cranky. And that scared the heck out of him. Mainly, because he didn't *know* what to feel when he was with her, other than warm, strangely contented and more aroused than at any other time in his life.

Caring? He didn't do that. He hadn't done that for a very long time.

He was losing his edge.

'Hey! Steady. I do have a few morals, I'm sure…somewhere…' He patted his pockets as if trying to locate them. 'Just not the ones you want me to have. I do charitable deeds. Isn't that enough?'

She pulled even further back. 'You do charity? Which one? Over-sexed Rock Stars Anonymous? You know, with your money you could do a great deal to help kids like Marshall.'

'I've been thinking about doing more, and I will. I just need to get a few things sorted out. I'll look into it when I get back home.'

Spending time with her and those choir kids had opened him up to other ideas too. Maybe it was timing; the end of a tour that had sucked his energy, the chance to rethink where his life was going, or maybe it was just her. She made him want to clean up his act.

The frown that had been hovering over her forehead all day returned, just when he'd thought he'd erased it.

'So what else do you do in LA? When you're not busy being rich and famous?'

'I'm away touring for nine months, maybe a year, at a time and I'm usually pretty beat up when we're done. I work hard but then I need to let off steam and play hard. Very hard. Sometimes I get to take time out, like this, but usually we go from touring to the studio, a new album, then touring again. It's a bit like being a hamster in a wheel. Same old. Same old. But, as I say, I like to keep busy. It keeps me out of trouble.'

And only a few more days to go in exile and he'd be back on an even keel again. Maybe that was his problem—he was getting too used to the easy life, getting too used to… well, Sasha and her weird lists and her quirky ways, getting used to her soft folds and sweet smiles. He was getting too used to waking up with her every morning and the bright slash of lightness that burned in his chest.

Yeah, getting wasted in a different city every night would do him a power of good. There was nothing like stranger sex to make a guy forget a girl. But the more he thought about it, the less it appealed. Strange. 'Call me empty and shallow, but what you see is pretty much what you get.'

She shook her head. 'No. No, that's not true at all. I know you have this stage persona and then there's this other person. I think I've met him a couple of times. Briefly. Who is he?'

'Oh, you have questions? Go ahead.' He peered into her handbag and pretended to look for something. 'You want me to fill out a questionnaire? A checklist?' At the pursed lips and exaggerated frown he continued, 'No? Really, you are slacking, *list girl*. Let's start with the physical. I have full-working body parts, but then, you know that.'

'Oh…yes, I do. Full working order.' Her hesitant smile sparkled a little and grew as she drummed fingers on the table. 'A checklist. I can't believe I didn't think of that. Let me see, what would I be looking to ask?' Her nose wrinkled as he ran his fingers down her spine. 'Hey, I know, we could do a SWOT analysis.'

'Are you serious?'

'It couldn't hurt.'

He laughed. 'You are serious? Sasha—this isn't a bloody employment interview. Although, I do have a lot of strengths.' No way was he going to get sucked into any kind of self-analysis. He'd paid way too much to shrinks to be told he had commitment issues, he struggled with emotional attachment. Blah. Blah. Like every man he'd ever met.

He certainly struggled with something when Sasha was around. But usually it was the fact she was wearing way too many clothes. Today's dress was vintage black silk cocktail with thin straps that kept falling off her shoulder. Perfect for a sophisticated dinner out, but he wanted to rip the damn thing off her.

Sophisticated was hellishly overrated.

He nibbled across her collarbone, feeling her reluctant squirm, the softening of her muscles.

She giggled. 'Okay. So you're very good at that. Now, stop it…I'm being serious.' Serious with a devilish smile and a promise in her eye. He wanted her naked. Now. But she kept right on talking. 'How about hobbies, dreams, long-term plans…or your business strategies…pension scheme?'

'I think you'll find I'm financially secure.' Thank God something was, because his heart was dancing around like a firecracker. But so typical of Sasha that she'd consider a pension scheme in her tick list of qualities in a man.

'I much preferred talking about the physical, but as you're so insistent…I have fund managers and investors to deal with the fiscal side. I'm the creative one, but there are others, like Dario, the band, producers, stage management, roadies, choreographers, stylists, caterers, marketeers and the rest…It takes a lot of people to make a global brand work. And that's all I am in reality. A product. We have a lot of meetings, with bits of paper and folders and everything. You'd love it. If I gave it all up there'd be a lot of people without jobs.'

'Gosh, I never thought of it like that before—so many people dependent on your success. That's quite a weight to carry around.'

'I have broad shoulders.'

'Indeed.' She sighed, but she tipped her head to one side looking at him, eyes full of questions that he didn't think had much to do with this particular conversation. 'Okay, weaknesses?'

'None.'

'How about tall, blonde, big bazookas?'

'The girls?' He laughed, was she a mind-reader? He really hadn't thought about that kind of game for a while. Not since… He tried to think. Not since losing himself in rose-scented red hair and list-making had become his top two favourite pastimes. 'No. Not interested, at all. Looks like you're my only weakness.' Dangerous, yet compelling. 'And I can't think of any threats.'

He wrapped his arms round her and pulled her close. Then his hand ran along her thigh until she squirmed. But he held her tight, not allowing her to escape no matter how much she wriggled. He stole another quick kiss. 'And I make sure I always grab every opportunity.'

'Yes, yes.' She laughed, her shoulders relaxing and the shadows around her eyes melting a little. Her fingers tip-toed across his pecs. 'So which part of the Nate Munro product is the real you and which is fake?'

Leaning back in the leather seat, he clasped his hands behind his head and grinned. 'Believe me, sweet thing. I'm all real.'

'Idiot.'

He hadn't expected the thwack to his upper arm, but it hardly registered. 'Hey…and you've seen me naked. How much more real do you need me to be?'

'Nathan, half the women in California have seen you naked.'

'Good point. But I've never brought any of them here and I've never spoken to them about Marshall or my previous life—'

That truth jolted him. He was getting in too deep, opening up too many wounds. And she was getting too involved.

He shouldn't give her the impression she was any more special than the rest. He wasn't the guy she needed to fall in love with. He couldn't give her what she deserved, the promises bit, the stable home life bit. And it wasn't that he didn't want to live that kind of life at some point; he just didn't know how.

But somehow he just couldn't stop.

The heavy mahogany door creaked open and a waiter appeared with their food.

Sasha jumped and sidled to the edge of her chair, her cheeks reddening. 'You'd better go back to your seat, Casanova. The show's over and I'm starving.'

'Okay,' Nate whispered across the space, trying to deflect the ache that had settled in his chest, trying to make things light. 'Okay, I have an idea. Let's play a game.'

CHAPTER ELEVEN

SASHA SWALLOWED A mouthful of the most exquisite risotto she'd ever eaten, then leaned in. She liked to play. So long as they played safe. 'What exactly?'

'I name two things and you choose which one you prefer. See if we like the same things and if we're remotely compatible.'

'I already know we're woefully incompatible. If you're talking lists I could write one with all the reasons we shouldn't be doing this.'

'I'm sure you could, and probably already have.'

'Well, maybe. One or two.' She blushed; he'd certainly got the measure of her. But she was curious about his game. That couldn't hurt. Could it? 'Okay, then. Who goes first?'

A mischievous grin settled on his very sexy lips. 'Me. Easy start: which super power would you prefer to have—telepathy or X-ray vision?'

She laughed. 'And I thought this was going to be sensible. Typical male question. To read minds or see through clothes? Let me guess, you'd prefer X-rays, right?'

'Oh, yes. I don't think I want to know what's going on in any woman's head the whole time. But I'm guessing you like that kind of thing?'

She laughed and muttered into her glass of white wine, 'See? Chalk and cheese.'

'Sorry, is that a question? Because that's not how it works. The choices have to be kind of the same but—'

'Don't be stupid.' She stifled another giggle. No matter how hard she tried to be serious and get her sensible point across the man blocked her. Every time. 'I was just saying we're like chalk and cheese. So very different in every way. And please don't give me that awful opposites attract gumbo.'

'Are you sure you don't already have telepathy? Because that is exactly what I was thinking.' He raised his palms towards her. 'No, don't answer that. Telepathy doesn't exist.'

'When I was little I thought my mum and dad had it. They finished each other's sentences, knew what the other was thinking...'

But that wasn't true and she knew it now. Growing up, she'd believed her parents had the best of marriages and that her father had killed himself because he couldn't bear to let the woman he loved down, that he'd been brave and proud and that was why he'd left them.

But now, with more experience of people's hearts and minds, she wasn't so sure. Maybe her parents hadn't been soul mates after all. Maybe they'd just been two ordinary people who'd had arguments and compromised and muddled through. Maybe it wasn't that her father had loved them too much, maybe he just hadn't loved them enough.

Because if he'd truly loved them with all his heart, why had he done what he did? That wasn't brave, that was... hard. So very bloody gut-wrenchingly hard. 'At least that's what I always thought. I'm not convinced at all now though.'

Nathan's hand covered hers and she let his warmth rush through her. 'Hey, things between two people are never what they seem to the outside world, Sasha. There's always an element of pretence, a front.'

'Don't I know it? Seems to me that everyone's hiding something. So it's pretty hard to work out what the truth is.'

'I guess that's why you don't give your heart easily.'

'Trust has to work both ways as far as I'm concerned. And I'm done with trying to second-guess everyone.'

Her father's death, Nathan's story, even hearing it a decade later was mired in complex emotion and, if not deception, then a woeful lack of truth.

But then, she'd been as guilty as everyone else in holding things back. She was too frightened of the fallout.

The main course finished, Nate sat back and studied her. 'Do you want to talk about it? About your mum and dad?'

'No, thanks. You know that's off limits. And ancient history.' She refused to look him in the eye and let him see the shadows she knew were there, or pay attention to the sudden fist of pain in her ribcage. So she quickly changed the subject. Forced a smile that came easily when she looked at him. 'Back to the game. That's far more fun.'

He shrugged, his body freezing, his jaw tightening. 'Another time, then.'

Never. 'Starter or dessert?'

Even though she knew her refusal annoyed him, she couldn't lose even more of herself to him.

He looked as if he was consciously trying to relax, stretching out his fingers. 'I usually prefer a starter, but here they make the best *struffoli* in Italy. So I'd have to go with that.'

'Sounds like it should be a musical term. *Play the piece allegro with struffoli.*'

His mouth creased into a small smile. 'That would be very messy seeing as they're sticky balls of dough, covered in honey. Delicious. We should get some.' Ringing a bell, he caught the waiter's attention and started a little debate between the staff. 'Apparently they're only usually served at Christmas and for celebrations, but they're willing to make an exception. It may take a little time.'

She laughed, rolling her eyes. 'Of course. How marvellous to have everyone at your beck and call. Anything for you. Mr Wonderful.'

'Apart from you. Why don't you make an exception too, Sash?' His voice deepened, more a command than a question. 'Tell me.'

'No. Just no.' It wasn't her way. She'd kept everything shut down for so long, and her family wouldn't thank her for sharing their shame and their heartache. Her mother didn't need to go through that again. And Nathan lived too much in the public eye and too little in private; she didn't want to risk telling him anything if there was a chance it might ever get out again.

And, really, she was too damned scared to relive it all again.

'I'm sorry, but I'm not going to ruin a lovely evening.'

Heart pounding, she angled across the table and changed the subject the only way that worked with Nate Munro. She kissed him.

Long and hard and fast. Greedy, bold and powerful, meshing her lips to his, taking exactly what she needed, and giving him more in return. It certainly shut him up.

She pulled back and rubbed her hands together. 'Okay, back to business. Your turn for the preference game. Hit me with it.'

Surprise flickered across his eyes. 'You know, you're the only woman who's ever turned me down?'

Twice. No, more than that. Refused to share her pathetic life story. Refused to make love with him so many times she'd lost count and held him to a solemn promise that had taken ten years to follow through.

Her smile widened. It had been worth the wait. Every single second. It wasn't something she'd ever regret, even though watching him go would be so very hard. Chesterton was her reality and she wanted to live out a fantasy just a little while longer. 'And it's about time someone did. It's good for you. You shouldn't be able to have everything you want. You need to suffer once in a while, and learn to ask nicely. Oh, and to wait a little, not have everyone jumping around after you. It's what normal people do. It's character forming.'

'I have enough character as it is.'

'Too true. Way too much.' And every inch of it to die for, if not slightly maddening. 'Now, Mr Superstar, next question: if you can't think of one, then let me. Pool or ocean?'

He thought a while and rubbed a hand over his stubbled jaw. 'I have both, so it's a tough choice. Surfing versus boring laps? Saltwater versus disgusting chlorinated. Ocean's winning so far, I have to admit. But right now...Here? Definitely the pool.' His eyes heated; little flecks of gold sparked in the dark caramel. 'And a chance of skinny dipping...'

Another thing to tick off her bucket list. She laughed. 'Maybe...if you're good and ask nicely and wait a little...I could be convinced.'

'Sweet thing, I'll wait as long as you want. So long as it's about ten seconds.' He slid back into the seat beside her, his fingers stealing their way to her thigh, where he pressed his palm down hard, his thumb dangerously and enticingly too close for comfort.

The pressure was electric, sending spasms of need through her every nerve cell. She twisted to face him, her breath coming in tight gasps. She couldn't deny him, couldn't refuse him. Skinny dipping it was. Plus a whole lot of everything else.

Maybe telepathy did exist after all, because right now she knew exactly what was going on in his mind. 'You want to get the *struffoli* to go?'

'Fast or slow?' Nathan whispered into Sasha's ear as he finally found the strength to let go of her. She'd come through on the skinny dipping, and more. So much more. And holding her, inside her, watching her lose control again and again, tipping over the edge, had been the most sensual thing he'd ever done.

She shifted underneath him, breathless and satiated, pulling faux-fur blankets over them as they lay on the sun lounger in the dark.

'Hmmm, tricky.' She sighed, her breath like a gentle kiss on his neck, her curves fitting against him like a hand in a glove. A perfect fit. 'Either. Both. So long as it's with you…' Her hand cupped his cheek as she gazed at him. 'Eyes or mouth?'

Man, he loved this game. It cut through the crap and got down to the heart of things.

He loved the aftermath of great sex too, the fading glow, the deep relaxation it brought, the soft purr of satisfaction that rippled through his muscles.

And with a zillion stars winking at him through the silver slash of the Milky Way, a beautiful woman slick and wet from their midnight swim wrapped in his arms, it was as if he'd been teleported to a wild out-of-this-world film set.

'A man should never have to make a choice like that. Your eyes are amazing, but your mouth…' He groaned into the tumble of red curls, remembering the things her mouth had done to him…He groaned. 'Sasha, your mouth should be X-rated. Your mouth should never be allowed in Chesterton High again. Your mouth—'

But before he could finish she'd filled his mouth with her taste, her tongue. Soft and yielding, her kiss was filled with something that made his heart stutter.

She pulled away, tied her silk robe loosely round her waist, laid her head back on his shoulder and looked up at the sky. 'Heart or brain?'

'Whoa, Sasha. That's the biggest question in the universe. I wish I could say heart. But truly? You've got to go with brain every time.'

'Why?'

'Because otherwise you get sucked in by sentiment, make poor choices. I've been doing that way too long. It's got to be brain.'

She sighed. 'Disappointing then, given that we're lying here, doing this.'

'Believe me, if I'd led with my heart I'd have had you that first night. In the limo.'

'That would have been leading with your groin. There is a difference.'

'Huh? Really?' Yes, he knew that. But looking back it was the same thing. Heart, brain and body, all bowled over when the Sasha tornado hit. She was smart, funny, sexy and not interested in his fame or money. She had a huge heart and brought out the best in people. She was…well, goddamn it…she was perfect.

For the settling kind of guy. But instead of relief he felt a strange sense of regret, the slow thud of his heart as it contracted.

She turned her face up to him and her smile just about undid him. He scrambled around for some kind of distraction before he did or said something stupid. 'Okay, so this brings me nicely onto: romance or…er, horror?'

Seemingly oblivious to the effect she had on him, she bit the corner of her lip and he fell just a little bit deeper under her spell. 'I've had my fair share of one and not enough of the other.'

'Okay, don't say any more, I don't think I want to know about how many men have tried to win your heart. Or how many times you've given them it.'

'I wasn't saying I'd had a lot of romance. I meant I'd had enough of horror.'

'I guess teaching teenagers can do that to you, Miss Sweet.' But she was serious. Her body stiffened and the chill air drifted into the spaces that had been filled with their heat. This was the in-road he'd been waiting for. So he grabbed it. 'Now's a good time, Sasha.'

'No. I'm fine.' She didn't even ask what he was talking about, but she knew.

'Really?'

'Yes. Yes. Absolutely.' The upturn in her lips was a poor attempt at a smile.

'So why the fake smile? I can spot one at fifty paces. Don't forget, sweetheart, I'm usually surrounded by them.' Memories of their break-up night swam back to him. She'd been on the brink of telling him, finally, but then she'd held back. Refused to share the one thing that had driven a wedge between them, the reason she wouldn't ever trust him wholly. 'Ten years you've kept this from me. More. Stop trying to be so tough.'

'I'm not trying to be tough. I just don't want to go there.'

He huffed out a breath, trying not to sound too angry when all he wanted was to be angry. Angry with who he wasn't too sure.

'Really? Over it as in your body reacts instinctively at the mere thought of whatever it was that hurt you? Over it as in you can now willingly, honestly and openly allow yourself to start trusting people?' He paused, took control of his rippling anger, subsuming the feeling of betrayal. 'Do you even want to?'

'Of course. Of course I do.' She inhaled deeply then shuddered out the breath. 'You're a good man, Nate Munro, whatever anyone prints about you. And if I was going to talk to anyone about it, it'd be you…'

And that was a screwed-up sucker punch to his heart. He'd been called a lot of things in his career, but *a good man* was never one of them. But he was clearly not good enough. 'If I'm that damned good why can't you talk to me?'

A pause lengthened between them as the breeze dropped,

leaving nothing but the sound of their breathing cutting through the night.

'The truth is…I'm scared to say it out loud. Because that way it makes it real all over again.' Her lips trembled as she thought. After a second or two she nodded. 'I suppose if you looked hard enough you could find out anyway. It was big news back then. *Mr Business fails spectacularly.*' The laugh in her voice was sarcastic and cold, just like the breeze settling over the night.

Eventually she turned over onto her back and stared up at the sky. 'Okay…Well…you know my dad…committed suicide?'

'Aha.' His heart pounded hard and loud. Nate didn't want to speak, didn't want to stop her from purging herself of whatever it was that had formed the essence of this strong yet vulnerable woman.

But he was scared too. Scared for her, scared that she'd had to endure something that was clearly very ugly. So instead of speaking he held her, his throat raw with the pressure of the unknown, nodding slowly into her hair as she shook. Waiting for the fallout.

He didn't have to wait long. Her voice was so small that he had to strain to hear it.

'I was the one who found him.'

CHAPTER TWELVE

'I WAS TEN years old, craving attention from a daddy who'd changed over the months from being kind and attentive to silent and reclusive.'

How had it got to this? Fast, slow. Black, white. Secrets, lies. Past, present.

Sasha took another breath. It seemed there'd never be enough air to squeeze down her fast-closing throat. Repressed images from that night flickered through her brain like a bad old movie while deep inside a rising panic threatened, but she swallowed it back.

'He was in his study staring blankly out of the window. And I wanted my old happy dad back so I scuttled in and tried to sit on his knee, asking if he could help me get my bike from the back of the garage. But he pushed me away and shouted that he was too busy. That I was selfish and spoilt. He yelled and yelled, getting more and more worked up. Then…he did something he'd never done before…'

Even now after all this time she couldn't believe it. Sure, she'd rationalised his motives, but the actual physical act had been so unlike the father she'd grown up with. 'He hit me. A loud smack across my face that sent me reeling to the floor. Hard and sharp and thick on my cheek.'

She could have sworn the sting flared again as she touched her face. Nate's hand followed and he grasped her fingers in his fist, his touch spurring her on.

'And he just kept staring at me, grey with horror, as if unable to understand what he'd done, saying, *"I'm sorry. I'm sorry. I'm sorry."* Then he rushed out of the room.'

'Some people react badly under pressure.' Nate squeezed her hand. 'I should know.'

'But my upbringing was nothing like yours, Nate. I didn't know violence. My life had been a fairy tale until then, although I'd always thought it was boringly normal. Then he changed. I was scared. Everything seemed to be unwinding out of control.'

'And then…?'

'I heard my sisters laughing and chatting downstairs. My mum working in the kitchen. The slam of the garage door. A car backfiring in the street.'

'Only it wasn't a car?' Nate's voice was quiet and gentle.

She shook her head, inhaled deeply, unsure if she could continue. Tears stung the backs of her eyes, but she refused to let them fall. 'No. It wasn't. But I didn't know that. I'd heard the garage door and I headed there for my bike, thinking he'd gone to get it for me.'

'Oh, God…but he hadn't…'

For some reason her leg had started to jitter, up and down, up and down. She couldn't stop it. It beat a wild, out-of-control rhythm.

And there was Nate's palm resting a light pressure on it to slow it down. For once, the steady to her chaos and, God knew, she needed him right now. Needed this. Needed his arms around her, his chest to lie against, his heart to pump a regular rhythm she could follow.

'A smell hit me; weird, smoky, metallic, pure, but terrifying. And no noise. Nothing at all, not even the sound of his breathing. But there he was. So much blood over everything. And over me eventually, when he wouldn't wake up. And then my mum was behind me, telling me to come back into the house with her.'

'I'm so sorry you had to go through that, Sasha.'

'Me too.' She was suddenly cold through to her bones. So cold.

Nate's eyes closed for a moment. When he opened them they were tormented. 'But why? Why would he do that?'

'He'd put all his money into a pension company that failed. His business partner—his best friend—disappeared with all the cash, leaving Dad to face the creditors. He'd tried to protect us, but there was hate mail, a pending court case, prospective jail time, and massive media coverage, journalists at the door braying for his blood.' She couldn't stop the bitter laugh. 'Well, they got it.'

Nate shifted as he became more animated, his hands raised and his fists clenched. 'But why didn't he face them all? Fight them? Why did it have to be so...?'

'Final? Violent? Cowardly? Afterwards I thought it was cowardly to leave us all. But Daddy had never been a coward. He was strong and honourable and always did the right thing. Whatever made him take his own life must have been a dark force that overwhelmed him.'

She sank further into Nate's arms, taking comfort from his heat. 'But he was a broken man too. Trust came too easily to him and he couldn't believe what had happened. Eventually it must have become too much for him to cope with. I guess, faced with all that, it seemed the only way out.'

And yet getting over his actions had held her and her family prisoner for the rest of their lives, in one way or another.

Over the years she'd worked hard to erase the images from her head, shutting the door on that part of her life. But the scars were there still, she now realised, dressed up in her inability to allow herself to dream or to relax, or, indeed, to trust anyone not to do something so extreme again.

Laughable really. She hated extremes and chaos. Yet

here she was opening her soul to the human embodiment of them.

His fingers stroked down her back. 'But instead of wallowing in it, or taking your anger and grief out on the world, you became a teacher and give so much to everyone. And you never ask for anything in return.'

'The way I see it, school was my constant, the one thing I could rely on to be the same every day. No surprises, just routine where I felt safe and could leave the chaos of home behind. And, to be honest, there were some pretty decent adults who wanted the best for me. If there's one kid at Chesterton High who needs that, then I'm there for them. Plus, channelling energy into something positive is empowering too…A bit like sex.'

She'd never realised how powerful a woman could become when she let her sexual instincts take over. How liberating letting go could be. It had only taken seventeen years for her to understand. Heck, she was a slow learner.

But now she had a good teacher and the things his hands could make her feel…

'Now that I can understand, sweet thing. Sometimes you surprise even me.'

His knuckle ran across her cheek, then his mouth followed, tracing tiny kisses over her lips, her cheeks, the nub of her nose, her eyelids. Back to her mouth where he pressed his lips against hers and she opened to him, safe and warm in his arms.

Here was a man who would face bad times—*had* faced bad times, and would fight back with everything he had. Bare knuckle if need be, but he'd fight.

His life might well be played out in public, but his love was kept so preciously and deeply private.

He tasted sweet and soft and of hope. And at that moment she knew she could truly fall for him. Hard. She could learn to love him too, perhaps, given some time and a chance. Maybe she already did. Because how could she not?

The pain in her chest melted slowly, overwhelmed by something else, something equally weighty, but not as devastating, or as hollow. Eventually he pulled away and offered Sasha his hand to stand. 'I think it's time we went inside and worked a bit more on Sasha-empowerment, don't you?'

'Most definitely. And this time I get to call the shots.'

'Oh, God, I've unleashed a monster.' He laughed. 'We've got all night. And the next…'

Wrapping a blanket around her shoulders, he took her hand, and walked her up the terracotta steps towards his amazing terracotta castello. A bright silver moon illuminated the endless fields of vines casting an ethereal glow, almost magical. Here, she figured, anything was possible. Even talking about something she'd never mentioned to a soul. Or maybe she'd been lucky with finding the right person to listen.

She followed him past the library, the dining room, into the opulent lounge, breathing in the reassuring centuries-old aroma of polished wood mixed with new vine growth, eucalyptus, fresh air.

'Here, have this, it'll make you feel better.' He gave her a glass of something from a crystal decanter. Thick and dark, it burnt her throat but it hit the spot. Almost immediately the horror started to fade, replaced by a warmth deep in her gut.

He took a big gulp, then looked at her, brows furrowed. 'Just one thing. Why didn't you tell me this all those years ago? Why keep something like that bottled up?'

'I was raw and damaged. Would it have made a difference?'

'I don't know. I'd like to think I'd have tried to help you work it out. I guess my efforts would have been clumsy, but I always felt you were holding something back from me. Something that stopped you trusting me. You remember that last day? You were quiet at school, but I knew there was something bothering you. You refused to talk about it, and...'

'Because I wouldn't trust enough to confide in you, you went looking for a fight. And you got one.'

He was right. However much she dressed up her insecurities in organisational perfection and her, quite literally, uptight approach to sex, it all amounted to her holding everyone at arm's length. Even to the point of pushing him to his limits. And losing him in the process.

'And now you know why. We moved to Chesterton to get away from all the attention. My mum was sick from the stress. She refused to talk about it and tried to put on a brave face. We all did. I packaged everything up and pushed it deep inside myself as far as it would go. In a matter of months our happy ordinary life was ripped apart—everything I knew had changed and bowled out of control. Not talking about it made me feel like it couldn't possibly have happened.'

'So you micro-managed everything. If you controlled things, things wouldn't get out of control. Right?' He smiled gently, pinning a rogue curl of hair behind her ear. 'Those lists. The reluctance to just pack up and leave.'

'I guess so. I was only ten and I didn't think like that. It was more like, if I behaved well and made sure I planned everything then nothing bad would happen.' She smiled. 'The OCD just developed.'

'And the trust thing?'

Oh, yes. She took another sip as she thought, bought some time. 'The million-dollar question? Trust comes hard when you see what can happen. I'm working on it. But then sometimes there's this little voice in the back of my head asking: *what if something so bad happens again*? And that sense of threat tarnishes everything. It makes you see the world differently, takes away your ability to get close to anyone.' She noticed the glass shaking in her hand and fought to steady herself. 'You're just waiting for it all to fall apart again. And what if it does?'

It took a long time for his answer to come. He peered down into his drink, as if the crystal held all the answers in the universe. When he finally spoke his voice was the most serious it had ever been, his eyes burning with a fierce passion. 'Then I'll be there for you. I'll catch you, Sasha. I won't even let it happen in the first place.'

He believed it so fervently she almost allowed herself to believe him too.

But she wouldn't get carried away. They only had a few short days left and she was under no illusion what was going to happen at the end. 'Well, don't dare treat me any differently, Nate. One show of pity and I'm gone.'

He brought her to an ornate antique chaise and sat down, pulling her onto his knee. 'God, sweet thing, I don't pity you at all. I've been through some stuff, but it's nothing compared to you. Big respect. As Dario would say, you're one seriously cool chick.'

'Aww, he's got such a way with words.'

'Well, I'm not about to let him loose with any lyrics just yet, but he's right. So, so right.'

And then he held her on his knee, slowly stroking her hair. The mantelpiece clock ticked sonorously on and on as liquor and a solid pair of arms eased her transition from a nightmare past back to the present.

For how long they stayed there she didn't know. But it was enough. Enough to send the ghosts shivering back to where they came from, unable to hurt her any more. Enough to give her time to adjust to the new Sasha she could be now that her secrets had been unlocked.

She straddled his lap and leaned forward to press a kiss

onto his forehead, his cheek, his lips. Ran her hands down
his sculpted sun-tanned chest. 'So, we have four more days,
Nathan Munro, and I'm really out on a limb here with no
schedule and no planner, pushing all my trauma issues to
the limit. So you'd better make it worth my while, d'you
hear?'

Her bikini bottoms were no barrier to the warmth of his
skin and the sudden shock of his physical reaction to her.

Four days. That was all they had left and she was going
to make the most of it. Because she wanted him now, and
she was through with living scared. She'd deal with the
consequences later.

A buzz of renewed desire prickled over her, a reawak-
ening of her innate reaction every time she saw him. 'Kiss
me? Take me to bed? Surprise me? Let me surprise you?'

This time when his lips crushed hers they were ardent
and heated. Gone was the soft caressing, replaced now by
an urgency that deepened with every stroke of his tongue.
Something fundamental had changed between them and
it showed in the way he tasted, the intense way he gazed
at her, a new respect. A deeper connection. Deepening all
the time.

'God, Sasha, you've been through hell and missed out
on so much loving.' His hands slid the length of her back,
stopping briefly to untie the strings on her bikini, then
he cupped her bottom, groaning as she rocked against his
erection. 'And I'm going to spend the next few days making it up to you.'

CHAPTER THIRTEEN

AND HE'D BEEN as good as his word, Sasha mused as she dragged her eyes away from Nate and watched the London skyline come into view.

A tight knot settled in her chest. The last few days had passed in a blur of long delicious lunches in remote ancient villages, hair-raising scooter rides under bright blue Tuscan skies and endless sunshine, not to mention the journey of sexual discovery he'd taken her on.

To say she'd been liberated was an understatement. Every inch of her had succumbed to the Nate Munro treatment and he'd sensationally shown her how to express her feelings through touch.

Particularly last night. Their last night. Which had passed in a heart-wrenching blur that she had never wanted to end, of alternating laughter and long pauses where they'd simply looked at each other, a world of emotion passing between them. How could they get so lucky to have found each other again? To have shared this incredible time together?

But they'd made no plans past this day. This hour. And her brain was starting to feel like a rudderless boat, going round and round in circles. The reality of their very different lives was evident in this private jet, the crystal champagne flutes and very personal attention.

'Mr Munro, Miss Sweet, please fasten your seat belts

for landing.' The air stewardess flashed a plastic smile at Sasha and a very open and genuine one to Nate. 'Captain Walsh says he's secured you a seat on the two-thirty to LA. It'll be a bit of a squeeze, time-wise, but there'll be a car at Denham waiting to take you to Heathrow.'

Time was going too fast. Sasha's stomach tightened. She tried not to look too possessive as she gripped his hand through the turbulence that heralded their descent through thick grey clouds.

But for the last few moments of their trip she wanted to savour him and she was almost past caring who saw her. 'So it's welcome back to the real world, then, Nate. I think I'm going into culture shock already.'

His brows lifted but his beautiful face became a mask of impartiality. Sasha got the feeling it was because of the air-crew, so protective was he of his emotions, but she couldn't help thinking she was losing him already. 'Reality has to hit some time, baby. We can't hide away for ever.'

Baby? Back to his act now? Rock-star-speak not Nathan-speak. The walls were building brick by brick with every metre the plane descended. While frustration and hope-lessness nibbled away at her insides. 'Can't we? More's the pity.'

He frowned. 'I thought you loved your job?'

'I do, absolutely. I have the competition coming up and I have to work on that for a start. I just wish…oh, never mind.' After so many hours of being open and honest with him she couldn't find the words to express her feelings now. Yes, she wanted her old life back, but she wanted something more now too.

She wanted him. A future with him.

The real him he'd allowed her to see, the Nathan Munro who had wrapped her in his arms and listened to her story, who made her laugh, made her heart soar. Who made her believe she could be so much more. Free. Alive. Wanted.

Even though the 'L' word had been mentioned ever so casually it had never been said in that momentous way she imagined it should be. *I love you.*

No. Neither of them had ever said that, but she could have. Despite all her efforts she had fallen hopelessly in love with him. No slippers, no family saloon, no promises for ever. Not even a plan past tomorrow. Mr Absolutely, Very Definitely, Heart-Stoppingly Wrong In Every Way.

I love you.

The urge to shout it almost drove her mad. Was it so selfish to crave something so utterly precious, yet so undeniably unsafe? But she'd learnt from her father's suicide that even the most secure things could become broken.

Old Sasha might well have sat back and planned how to mend her broken heart, but new Sasha was going to try and work out a way they could both have their dreams, their lives. Somehow.

She'd spent too long looking at the world with fear-filled vision. Lived life in the shadow of her father's death. She didn't want to be scared any more. She didn't want to take what made her safe. She wanted to take what made her happy.

Nathan Munro.

She would tell him she loved him. She would work out a plan for them both.

Her heart thumped loud and hard. She felt as if she were on the edge of a precipice dredging up the nerve to jump— absolute fear and exhilaration mingling in her blood.

Then the plane jerked to a halt. The air stewardess spoke to them again. Nate reached for his bag. Chatted to the pilot.

Before she knew it they'd hit the stairs and were breathing fresh English air, the sound of her voice drowned out by aircraft engine and a cruel northerly wind.

I love you.

As they crossed the tarmac to the terminal building he

gave her a weary smile that almost broke her heart. He took her hand, more in an effort to speed her up, she thought, than in any kind of romantic gesture.

'Right, Sash. So you have to be at school first thing tomorrow morning. And I'm getting the next flight to LA. I have to do that interview and a whole bunch of promo for my new album. Come on, we have to keep moving.'

Damn. Damn. Damn. Why the harsh tone? He was hurting her.

But Nate couldn't help himself. He'd spent the best part of a decade learning how to be someone else, especially in public, and he couldn't shake that off. Not even for her. And he had no way of coming to terms with how he felt. He didn't even *know* how he felt. Apart from that something important was coming to an end and he didn't know how to stop it, and that if he didn't act soon he'd lose her for ever.

He caught her arm as they entered the tiny private airport transit hall; once outside the other end they would both be going home. Not together.

He couldn't fathom the screwed-up twisting in his chest. It hurt. Actually hurt. He loved going back to LA. Going home. Loved it. But now? He couldn't contemplate that big empty space in LA, and Sasha in her shoebox, here.

His throat was raw. Every bloody emotion had bundled up in his ribcage and he had to keep hauling in air just to stay upright.

He wanted to say something to make everything right. But what? He didn't know what right was. He hadn't promised her anything after all. 'Hey, look, Sasha. I'm sorry—'

A bright flash made them turn towards the immigration desk. Further along the corridor he saw a group of photographers he recognised from countless times before. The ones that took the risks, but got the shots.

And then he saw Sasha's eyes darken. 'How did they know we were here? It's a private airfield.'

That sharp ache in his chest? Just got a whole lot worse. He pulled her closer. 'Someone will have told them. And if I find out who…'

'Nate! Sasha! Sasha Sweet!' One of the men stepped forward and clicked. *'Are you taming our bad boy?'*

'Sir, your cab is waiting. Your flight is leaving soon.' An airline representative pressed into his face. 'Sir. Mr Munro. We have to—'

'Where's Security? We're not stepping foot out there,' he rallied back at the staff member.

'I've radioed them, sir. I don't know where they are. They should be here. They're always here. I can only apologise.'

'Too right. This is ridiculous. How did they even get in here?'

'Sasha! Tell us about your father.'

'What?' Sasha glanced angrily from the airline rep to Nate, to the photographers, clearly trying to come to terms with the intrusion. 'Er…no comment.'

'Don't dignify their presence with one word. They're not worth it.' Nate pressed a finger to her lips, determined not to rise to their bait. While his fists balled.

He ignored the tightening in his chest, and kept his voice steady for Sasha. 'Let me sort it out.'

'Why did he screw those people out of their pensions?'

His focus narrowed to that one sorry excuse for a man. 'What did you say, pal?'

'William Sweet. CEO of Sweetly Secure Finances. Screwed a lot of people out of a lot of money.'

He took a step forward. 'Where do you get off with this kind of drivel? Hey?'

Judging by the hack's quick retreat against the wall, he knew he'd crossed a line in gutter journalism.

Something inside Nate snapped.

So yeah, he'd made a promise not to get riled by these guys. Yes, he'd made a silent vow to curb his angry outbursts in front of Sasha. To even let it all wash over him. But that all faded into nothing in the face of her being dragged into this bloody circus.

The blood left Nate's fingers as he squeezed them tight. This was all his fault.

The one thing he'd said he'd do—protect her—and he couldn't. Disappointment didn't cut it.

But rage did.

It started as a deep ache in his gut, rose like bile to his throat, then rushed through him.

Without thinking he vaulted over the desk, grabbed the camera by the lens and tried to pull it away from the man. Nate's hand caught in the strap and suddenly he and the reporter were collapsing to the floor. As they fell he heard running footsteps, loud voices.

Finally. Security.

'Nathan.' But it was Sasha he came face to face with, hands firmly on her hips, as he stood up. Somehow, she seemed taller, stronger, braver. Pure indignation sparked from her eyes, infusing him with immense admiration and sending a shot of fire to his groin.

She flashed him an understanding smile. 'Honey, you know we talked about this.'

God. Sasha's body pulsed with a powerful rush of adrenaline as she stared at the two men. No, as she stared at Nate.

The ripped muscles, the feral reaction, the intense heat in his eyes as he'd leapt the barrier in her defence, fired something primal in her blood. Pure anger whirled with flagrant desire inside her and now she wanted a piece of the action too.

Maybe she was mad. Or just free. Free from doing everything right, from following her rigid rules, from not making waves just in case she got hurt.

Because she was hurting already—at Nathan, for retreating back into his shell when there was a whole lot of things they still needed to say. Hurting that this was the way their week was going to end. In a brawl on the floor. Hurting that someone would dredge up her father's death and use it as a weapon against her.

'It's okay, really. I get that you're pissed off. I understand. It's a blatant intrusion of our privacy, especially here, where it's supposed to be private…But getting angry isn't enough. Getting even is.'

'Too bloody right.' Nate stepped forward, but she stopped him with her hand on his chest.

'No. Wait. I've got this.'

He swiped a hand over his jaw and raised his eyebrows. 'Okay. Go for your life, sweet thing.'

Out of the corner of her eye she saw the reporter shuffling backwards, but she stomped on the camera strap. Stopped him short. Felt the ripple of anger seep through her cells, her bones, her skin, and waited for it to grow enough to harness it.

Years of dealing with stroppy, surly, unruly teenagers had honed her for *this* moment. Years of being too frightened to step out of her box had honed her for *this* moment.

It was time to fight for what she believed in.

'You.' She pinned the reporter with her take-no-crap stare. 'You should be ashamed of yourself.'

The little man nodded.

'Everyone has a right to a little privacy, right? You want people prowling round your house? Stalking your mother? Your sister…'

He shook his head.

'Your daughter? Making their lives hell? Going through

their bins? Telling their secrets? Because everyone has se-crets, right? Even you?'

The weasel nodded again. Was that all he could do? He was like a puppet.

'You want me to start searching your history up?'

Now he was starting to look ill.

'I thought not. Because that would be crass, wouldn't it? Low. But I'm not like you. I don't stoop that far.' She stepped closer and lowered her voice, commanding every bit of his worthless attention. 'So take your camera and your lousy morals and your greed and your pathetic desire to destroy other people's lives and stick it…'

But before she could tell him exactly where to stick it he'd scrambled up and fled to the exit. Coward.

'Coward!' She chased him up the corridor and watched, with a great deal of satisfaction, as he disappeared into the car park.

Yes! God, that felt so good.

What a team. Now where was Nathan?

Nathan. Her heart stalled. Tears pricked the backs of her eyes. His flight. For a brief moment she'd forgotten he wasn't going to the same place she was. And there was still so much to say.

She turned to see him standing at the immigration desk flanked by a security guard and the airline rep. She could see by Nate's tense stance that he'd climbed further into that shell. The distance he'd put between them was way more than physical. Despite the passion he'd felt for her, despite everything they'd shared, it just wasn't enough to make him stay.

This was definitely the end. Of that she had no doubt. There was no fairy-tale ending about to happen here.

The after-effects of the adrenaline shot made her start to shake and suddenly she felt bruised and battered as if her heart had been punched right out of her. She walked towards him.

Did she have to fight for him too?

A tight fist of pain lodged in Nate's chest. Part pride, part desolation, all awe.

'Wow…Sasha, you're on fire,' he said gently, to the woman he now knew he absolutely loved with every part of his soul. The one who had made him whole again, who had glued back together those hollow pieces he'd been pretending were his heart for far too long. Loved her. Completely.

Which was why this next conversation was going to shatter it all over again.

She stared up at him, eyes brimming with tears. Her hands trembled as she placed a finger on his mouth. 'Don't say it. Just…don't.'

'Mr Munro.' The airport rep tugged at his sleeve. 'They're starting to board. There's just enough time.'

'Mate, give me a minute. There'll be another flight.' But never another moment like this, a last moment that he wanted to treasure.

I love you.

He understood what that meant now. That subtle soft melding of souls, the sharp crackle of electricity. Laughter. A certain scent. Respect. A bone-melting ache. A lot of paper, too, it would seem, and files and stickies and paperclips and lists. And now, absolute awe.

Yeah, he loved Sasha Sweet with every cell in his body.

She was strong, stronger than he was, and she'd just proved she didn't need protecting. She didn't need him. And, sad truth was, he had nothing else to give her.

She'd hate him for doing this. But he'd spent a good part of his life doing the wrong thing, now it was time to man-up.

And she would survive, after all. She'd survived the

worst kind of nightmare that put his problems deep in the shade, and grown into a beautiful woman.

He didn't know what to do with all this chaos swirling in his head, his body. He was way out of control.

That scared the hell out of him.

He looked deep into those navy eyes that melted his heart Every. Single. Time. 'I have to go. The flight's waiting.'

'That's it? Finished? You're not even going to try to make it work?' Hauling in a deep breath, she pushed her fist into his chest. 'All this…us…and that's it? *I have to go*?'

'Look at it logically. We both have jobs, futures, lives and responsibilities, thousands of miles apart. You hate my world and I don't…can't fit into yours. Opposites don't attract, they just circle each other for a while and inevitably they go in separate directions.'

Her fist grabbed his shirt and she twisted the fabric into a ball. 'So what now? Thanks for the memories? Will I hear about it all in a number-one hit?'

'I don't think so.' He took his life in his hands and ran a finger down her cheek, caught the first tear but didn't show her that he'd noticed. 'You really are wired.'

'One of us has to be.' She blinked. And again. And he just knew she was trying to stop the tears from falling. 'Because I happen to think what we have is pretty special. No—really once-in-a-lifetime special.'

'But it can't be for ever. I never promised you that.' Man, this was the hardest thing he'd ever done. By a long way. Burying his brother and his mother had broken him, but this…this was a whole other depth of loss.

I love you. He ached to say those words, but if he did he would only make things worse. Better for her to believe she was a temporary fixture in his life than permanently etched on his heart. Otherwise she might do something crazy, like convince him to stay. 'If you ever need anything, anything at all, make sure to come find me. Okay?'

'Sure.' She couldn't hide the catch in her throat, the crack in her voice. 'I hear the men's room is the best place to get you these days.'

He took her wrist, drew a small heart with his fingertip on the sensitive skin, something he used to do so long ago he'd forgotten, sending shivers through him and a lump to his throat. 'Okay. Okay. Goodbye, sweet thing.'

'Hey, well, at least this time you actually said goodbye.'

CHAPTER FOURTEEN

Not So Sweet Talkin' Woman!

Lobby group, Celebrities Against Media Intrusion (CAMI), found itself an unlikely new advocate yesterday in the guise of spirited schoolteacher, Sasha Sweet.

The apparently very private Ms Sweet, Head of Music at Chesterton High School, learned firsthand the perils of media fame when she landed at a northwest London private airfield, accompanied by rock star, Nate Munro. The notorious bad boy of rock, whose hits include platinum bestsellers 'Sweet Talkin'' and 'Sex Me Up', and his alleged new paramour, Sasha, were returning to London after a week's break at a secret hideaway.

Their attempt at a cloak and dagger arrival was scuppered when News.com reporter, Malcolm Price, tried to snap them leaving the airport hand in hand. But Miss Sweet, described by a former pupil as 'shy but strict', very definitely put Mr Price in the naughty corner as she rallied against him with a verbal attack on media intrusion...

...Ms Sweet, however, is no stranger to scandal. As the daughter of the CEO of maligned pension company...

...The hilarious outburst, caught on camera by an airfield employee, shows Ms Sweet jumping to Munro's defence as he rugby-tackles the reporter to the floor. She then wags her finger at Mr Price, no doubt threatening him with a week's detention...and a hundred lines...

JUST BRILLIANT. EXCELLENT. So much for girl power.

Sasha lay back in her bed and dropped the paper to the floor, unable to read the rest of the article again.

Stupid teary swollen eyes.

But she didn't need any kind of clear vision to see what an epic mistake she'd made. She should never have gone with him to Italy. Crikey, she shouldn't have sought him out in the first place, and she certainly shouldn't have acted in such an outlandish way. Even if it had felt right, and so good.

Glancing down at the crumpled tabloid, she sighed. But then, if she hadn't gone she would never have truly known what love meant, that you could feel safe with the most dangerous of men. You could finally open yourself up to trust and it felt amazing. That one man could give you the gift of self-belief and the courage to let go.

One man. Nathan. *Only ever Nathan.*

Damn him. Did he really have to break her heart into too many pieces all over again?

Her cellphone rang. *Cassie.*

Oh, hell. Drawing in a deep breath, she answered. 'Hi Cass.'

'Who are you and what have you done with my sister?' Her sister's laughter caught Sasha off guard. 'Have you seen the papers? You made front page, second and fourth. And the video's gone viral on the Internet. You go, girl!'

'Yes and it's all rubbish. So I said a few things—'

'A few? You were epic. You should see the comments...

sassy, sexy, siren. You've sparked a whole new debate about privacy laws. Famous people are lining up to endorse what you said. You're a legend!'

Sasha cursed. She didn't want to be a legend, she wanted to be left alone to wallow with her broken heart. 'But they raked all that stuff up about Dad again. I feel terrible. Have you spoken to Mum? Suzy? I can't get through to them.'

'Yeah. Suzy is not amused—she's been fighting off reporters at the hospital and it's interfering with her job. If you ask me she spends far too much time there anyway. The distraction will do her good. And Mum? She was surprisingly sanguine about the whole thing. Time heals and all that.'

Sasha hoped to God it did. If only time could move a little more quickly. She could do with a little healing. Okay, a lot of healing. Starting now. 'I was worried it might set her back. I remember what she was like…before. I couldn't bear to have her go through that again.'

'Hey, stop worrying.' Cassie's voice softened. She'd been protected by them all and knew few details about the circumstances of her father's death. 'It was a long time ago, Sash. I think she's truly moved on now. She'll get over this. And so will you.'

Maybe she was right—maybe Sasha was the only one still living with the effects of the past. Not any more. Nate had seen to that. 'Thanks. I'm getting there.'

'But hey, what does Mr Killer-ass think? Are you planning more secret hideaways? Can I come?'

'No.' *Gosh, that hurts.* Sasha blinked away more tears. She was done with crying over him now. 'He's gone back to the States.'

'But you're seeing him again. Right?'

'No.' Okay, so she wasn't quite done with the tears. She scraped back the wet hair stuck to her cheek.

Her sister gasped. 'So what happened? He's gone? Leaving you to face this mess?'

Sasha looked at the flashing answer-phone machine full of messages he'd left as soon as he hit the tarmac in LAX. The ones that said he'd got lawyers on to the newspaper. That he'd do everything he could to stop any more information getting out. The ones that didn't say he was coming back any time soon.

If he couldn't see that what they had was worth fighting for then it was his loss. 'I don't need anyone to help me. I'm fine without him.'

'So he has gone. For good?'

'Yep.'

'Oh, I'm sorry, sis. I'm sorry I suggested it, that I encouraged it. I just wanted you to have some fun.'

'I did. I really did. It was the best time of my life.' She sighed. 'But now I'm definitely saving myself for the slippers man. And I'm prepared to wait a very long time.' For a man who'd never touch her heart the way Nathan had.

Cassie's voice turned just a little too bright. 'So, focus on you. You are beautiful. Your body is curvy in all the right places. You have amazing eyes, a beautiful smile and a generous heart. You are funny and talented and have so much to give the right guy, you just need to get out—what are you laughing at?'

'It's okay, thanks, Cass, but you know me. I already have a plan.'

'And why doesn't that surprise me? Spill.'

'That reporter needed telling—they all do. I'll never forget the way Mum used to hide behind the curtains, the little notes they'd push through the letterbox. The lies. So I've decided I'm going to do an interview with someone reputable and put the world straight about what really happened to Daddy. Tell the truth about the business, his colleague, the suicide.'

Her sister whooped. 'I was wrong about you. You're one feisty chick. Are you sure you want to put yourself on the line like that?'

'You know what? I'm sick of hiding behind it. You never know, it might help someone…someone like me.'

And being angry felt a damned sight better than thinking about how much her heart had shattered.

Her throat almost seized up. 'It's time for us all to have a fresh start. They're always printing lies. Even Nathan gets his share of far-fetched stories. Instead of ignoring them I'm going to turn this whole experience into something positive.'

Once she'd found the strength to actually get out of bed.

Then she was also going to write a whole new bucket list. One that definitely didn't include falling in love.

The sad truth was, with his passion and her planning they could have done something amazing together, improved life for others like her, or people like Marshall. After everything they'd been through they could have been happy—the missing part of each other's hearts. If she'd been enough for him to want to stay. If he'd thought that what they had was worth truly fighting for. Clearly he didn't.

Which was a crying shame.

Because she did.

But even if she could turn back the clock she'd still fall in love with Nathan Munro again, in a heartbeat.

Dario's grin was as wide as his bullish shoulders as he greeted Nate from the glittering stage at the National Music Awards. 'So you just got how many awards?'

'Five.'

'And the night's not over yet…' Dario clapped him between the shoulder blades and took a slug of very expensive French champagne. 'You're at the top of the game, man. Top. Of. The. Game. Best album. Best single. Best male artist…'

Nate put this latest award on the table alongside the others and stared at them all in dismay. What was he doing putting on a show? Smiling and schmoozing.

Why? Because that was what he did. He acted his part and played the game, never showing who he really was or what things really meant to him.

'Yeah. Yeah. So I guess I should be happy. Right?'

'You're not?' At Nate's shrug Dario shook his head. 'You're not.'

'Think I'm getting old, buddy. This kind of gig doesn't give me the same buzz any more. It feels a bit hollow.' Without someone to share it with.

Okay. Without Sasha to share it. He'd messed up again and a zillion awards wouldn't make him feel like a better man, never mind best damned male.

'So what are you saying? What are you going to do?'

'I have no idea. But I'm through with playing the wild bad boy. People get hurt.' Mainly him, and those around him. Sasha.

She'd been the only one to see through the packaging to his core. And she hadn't found him wanting—she'd believed in the best of him. She brought out a side of him he didn't know he had.

'Ah, mate.' Dario grabbed his arm and dragged him out of the auditorium to the accompaniment of shushes and angry whispers. But what the hell? It didn't matter any more. None of this. 'Come with me.'

'What? What are you doing?' Nate shrugged out of Dario's grip, uninterested in playing games or getting laid. 'If this is another of your booty-calls, I'm out. I'm just not interested.'

'I know you're not. You haven't been interested in anything since you got back from London.' He grinned and affected a feminine voice. 'You don't call, you don't text…'

'Yeah. Yeah. I've been…distracted.'

'Well, you need to snap out of it. You're rude in interviews, lacklustre in the studio. You need to pull it together, man. Unless…' His oldest friend took out a smartphone and held the screen up to Nate. 'This is the reason?'

Nate's heart dropped to his boots as there, flickering to life, was a video of Sasha in some TV interview. Sweet, strong, courageous and so perfect it made his heart ache, she talked of her father's death, of the effects that had on her life. Of her family. Her love for her job and the importance of special-needs support. She was eloquent, beautiful.

Not once would she answer questions about their brief *affair*, as the journalist dubbed it. But he saw the pain in her eyes. The same pain he'd seen as he'd walked away. The same pain twisting his heart right now.

He missed her. Missed her smell, her smile, even the lists that drove him crazy.

'Classy lady. And she's got a big following out there now. Quite the lobbyist. She's changing things, Nate. Changing people's opinions about press freedom to walk all over your private life.' Dario's voice cut through. 'Sack me if you want to, but I'm going to say it anyway…I reckon you need to stop acting like an idiot and start getting serious about a few things too. Clean up your act. Stop pushing people away. Start letting people in.'

'What do you mean?'

'I'm not going to get all California psycho-babble on you, Nate. But you need to give people a chance to get to know you. I mean, really get to know you. You've got a chip there on that shoulder and you're hiding behind it.'

'Nah, this is me. I've never been any different. Nate Munro.'

Dario frowned. 'It's been ten years, Nate. I've watched

you drink yourself into oblivion, do everything to excess, push yourself deeper and faster into wine and women. And never once have you made a proper lasting connection. Not once.'

Wow, this was an eye-opener he didn't need. But Dario was right, Nate conceded reluctantly. He did push people away, unable to handle any kind of honest contact or emotion. He'd realised it in the art gallery when he'd looked round and seen strangers' eyes staring out of his so-called friends' faces. Living in some kind of wilderness where he was thinking, acting but not feeling. Not living, not really.

Wild, definitely. Sane? Not so much.

But Sasha challenged that. She fired feelings in him he didn't think were possible. Bright light feelings, strong deep feelings and a sense of belonging to something, to someone, something good. He'd never had that before.

But he hadn't been able to handle it, preferring not to feel anything, as he had for the last God knew how many years. Scared that he'd be consumed by the feelings, the inevitable pain.

And so he'd done what he did best.

Ran away. Came back to a place that now felt nothing like home. And she hadn't even been here but it felt empty without her.

Everything did.

He'd hidden behind excuses fuelled with alcohol and anger instead of facing up to reality. Shunned real intimacy. Pretended that living off the rails was fine, great even. That being damaged was like wearing a badge of honour. The act had become reality.

Facing Dario, he took a breath. 'Okay, I need you to set up a couple of urgent meetings with my lawyers for tomorrow morning, first thing. And then organise flights to London immediately after.'

'You think she's going to take you back after you walked away from her? Twice?'

Nate's gut tightened at the risk he was going to take. 'Hell if I know. But I have to try to convince her. I don't care what you say, I'm not backing down.'

'But London—?'

He leaned into Dario's face. 'Will you listen to me? Yes, London.'

'No, Dumbo.' Dario's finger prodded Nate's chest but he was shaking his head and laughing. 'You listen to me. Not London. Manchester.'

'What?'

'It's that music contest thing tomorrow. She won't be in London. She'll be in Manchester.' He shook his head. 'Thank God someone's kept an eye on things while you moped around the house with a sore head for two weeks.'

'You kept an eye on her?'

Dario shrugged, flashing a wry smile. 'Well, she kind of grew on me. And you were different because of her. In a good way.'

Manchester. He'd forgotten. Dario was right: he'd been too busy staring at the bottom of a liquor bottle to keep up with the days.

'Cheers, mate.' He grabbed his friend's big bear face between his hands and kissed his bald head. 'I owe you.'

'Yeah, yeah, I know. More than you can ever imagine.' Dario drew away, laughing. 'I just hope she's worth it.'

'Oh, she is. But first I have to find her.'

CHAPTER FIFTEEN

'THIRD PLACE GOES to No Limits, Chesterton High School!'

'Oh wow. Just wow.' *Oh My God.* Sasha couldn't hear her own thoughts above the screams and her hammering heart. It was more then she'd dared hope for. 'Quick everyone. Up onto the stage.'

A sea of faces came in and out of focus as she stepped up to accept the award and passed it around to the choir. Just to see their delighted faces made this moment the proudest of her life. They'd come so far and worked so darned hard.

It was just such a shame that Nathan couldn't be here to share it with them. After all, he'd done so much to get them there.

Her heart contracted a little. Too bad. It was his loss to have made such a difference and not even know.

She drew in air and tried to steady herself. Ever since he'd left she'd ricocheted from sheer joy at the memories they'd made to utter despair. And now she had to speak through a throat thick with emotion.

'Just a quick thank you to everyone who has helped in this wonderful achievement. You were very kind and gave of your time generously. We owe you a huge debt. Without a doubt we wouldn't have got here without you.'

She hoped, if Nathan ever saw this on the Internet, if he'd even bother to look, that he would know she meant him, more than anyone else. He'd given them all such a gift of self-belief; if only he could find it within himself.

A movement in the wings distracted her momentarily, but when she turned her head to look she couldn't see anything but blackness and the folds of open curtains.

Strange.

Focus.

'Er…and I wanted to say how proud I am of these wonderful gifted kids—'

Now the tiny hairs all over her body prickled, making her lose track of her speech. Great. She was going to be the laughing stock of the whole competition. *Teacher struck dumb at singing contest.*

But…something…

She glanced again to the side of the stage and saw the silhouette of a man. Proud jawline. The arrogant stance that told the world he didn't give a damn, when she knew he'd cared deeply.

But not deeply enough.

Nathan.

Her heart stalled as he caught her gaze. Every fibre in her body craved his touch; heat pooled in her abdomen then seeped out to her skin. Was he here for the show? The final act? But there'd been nothing on the programme about a special guest.

In which case…did that mean…? What she thought it might mean? That he was here for her? Her chest grew tighter and tighter.

Hello? An audience of three thousand…

Oops. She leaned into the microphone again. 'And… er…so…thank you to the organisers…' Damned dry mouth.

She looked over to him again. Was he meant to be presenting an award? Was he supposed to be up here too?

She raised her eyebrows to him in question. *What am I supposed to do now?*

He held up his palm and shook his head, urging her to continue her speech.

Great, all very well for you to say that now, Mr Hotshot. Now that I'm truly speechless.

The sea of faces started to look bemused. People began to shuffle, stare down at their shoes, whisper. *This was the teacher who made the news? Catatonic.*

Oh, hell.

'Er…and thank you all very much. Goodnight.' Stepping away from the microphone, she whispered to the choir, 'Very well done. Now we just have to go backstage to wait for the other announcements.'

While she either calmed down or got arrested for the murder of an infuriating rock god with an ass to die for.

I was provoked, Your Honour.

Wiping her sweaty palms down her dress, she walked off the stage on extremely shaky legs flanked by fourteen hyper-excited singers, who surged towards Nate giving high fives, squealing, jumping, pulling at his arms.

Above their heads he watched her, his eyes assessing, unsure, cautious.

Good.

It took a few moments to herd them into some kind of order, then he held out his arms to her as if she might walk straight into them.

Not a chance. 'Great timing, Mr Munro. Couldn't you have waited until I'd finished my moment of glory on stage? Now the world is going to think I haven't got a sensible brain cell in my head.'

He flashed her a grin that made him look devilishly handsome. 'No. I think I win that particular award.'

'Well, we knew that already.'

Wariness flickered across his eyes. 'Can we talk?'

'Sure, go right ahead.'

'Somewhere private?' *Please.* His eyes pleaded with her as he gestured towards the choir, whose heads bounced back and forth between Nate and Sasha as if watching a tennis match. 'Fourteen's a crowd?'

'Aren't you used to dealing with large audiences?' She folded her arms, enjoying every moment of his predicament. 'I can't leave them, and I'm sure they'd all love to hear what you have to say.'

'Yes! Yes! Yes!'

For someone so used to working with adoring fans hanging off his every word, he looked strangely sheepish. Pale even.

He coughed, his mouth tightening into a grimace. 'Okay. Well…That was…awesome, No Limits. Congratulations everyone. I've booked a couple of limos for afterwards and we're all going to go for a celebratory ride. Okay?' He pulled them into a tight huddle. 'Now, Miss Sweet and I have something very important to discuss, so go back to your seats and we'll be along shortly.'

'Are you going to kiss her?' It was George, the boy who reminded Nate so much of his brother. Lovely George. Knew all the right questions.

Nate looked right at her. Deep down into her soul, which did a little jig no matter how much she tried to stop it. 'Yes. If she'll let me.'

More whoops.

The folded arms clenched across her chest, she shook her head resolutely. 'No. He. Is. Not.'

'Well, no man kisses a lady, with an audience.'

A collective of shoulders drooped. 'Awww…sir…that's not fair.'

Silence descended as they disappeared back into the theatre.

Nate grew serious. She thought about kicking up more

of a fuss, but, what the heck? She should at least hear him out. Then she'd kick that sorry splendid ass.

'Sash, I came to apologise.'

'And so you should. But here? Now? When I have four-teen teenagers to chaperone?'

'I wasn't thinking straight. I thought—'

She blinked, trying to contain the hope rising in her chest. They'd been here before and it hadn't ended nicely. 'That what Nate Munro wants, Nate Munro always gets, right? I'm surprised you didn't hop up onto the stage there and then. Do a little song or something…just for me. Or make a cringing speech. A flash mob. A huge embarrassing gesture. That would've ensured a few headlines.'

'Some things are just better kept out of the limelight.'

His eyes were warm with flecks of gold. Or it could have been the reflection of the stage lighting. Either way, the effect was mesmerising. *He* was mesmerising, even at his most vulnerable, right now, out of his depth and yet still commanding every scrap of her attention.

A lump squeezed in her throat. 'Oh? What kind of things?'

'I love you,' he said, the words carrying the weight of his emotions, steady and true. 'From the second I saw you in Dario's arms, all feisty and fighting and flustered. I just didn't think it would be enough for us to overcome all these damned obstacles.' He stopped. Took a breath. Continued. 'And I was pretty damn stupid to run away.'

'Again.'

'Yes. Again.

'See, I've been running away for a long time—from myself, mainly. And then you came along again, out of the blue, making me feel things. Things I didn't want to feel. It was too intense. I wasn't ready for it—you were so fresh, so bright and then…so brave. So beautiful. You bowled me over. You bowled me right out of the emotional wasteland I'd been wallowing in and, wham—straight into full Technicolor feelings.' He smiled his just-for-her smile. 'I was scared. Terrified. I didn't want to feel those things. I didn't want to fall in love with you. I wasn't sure I even knew how—but you showed me.'

His arm wound round her waist and he edged her deeper into the folds of the black curtain backstage. Not in some brash Nate rock-star kind of way, but in a gentle Nathan kind of way. His closeness, his smell and heat wrapped around her like a cloak of safety.

'And—?' She should have said more, but the butterflies had hatched again in her stomach and were doing a crazy dance.

'I want to create a future with you, Sash. Somehow. You don't fit into my life and I don't fit into yours, so let's make a new one for ourselves. You and me.'

Her body screamed *yes*. But she held back. 'I can't. I just can't risk falling for you third time lucky. If you left me again I don't think I'd get out whole.'

'I won't leave you. I love you.'

He loved her.

She tried to ignore the emotions that threatened to overwhelm her. Yes, he was right, it was scary. But what was there in life that was really worth having, really worth taking a risk on, that wasn't just a little bit scary? If only she could believe that he actually meant every word.

'Since you left me *for the second time* I've got busy, quit my job. I'm going to live a little before I find Mr Right and settle down with my slippers and the safest car in Europe.'

'Mr Right?' Nate felt his fists clench… No other man would ever get the chance to touch her.

Stop.

Dragging in oxygen, he let his anger go and focused on loving her, even when she didn't want him to.

Stroking his hand over those breathtaking red curls, he told her, 'No one could love you more than I do. Heart and soul. You got me. I know I'm far from perfect, but I have changed. I want to be with you. I don't care about anything else. Answer me this—do you think you can love someone more than you love me?'

The pause gave him hope.

'No…Nathan. I don't. But I don't see how it can work.'

Nate's heart bounded up into his mouth. He'd blown the whole damned thing. He had to convince her that he was ready to fight for her, not with his fists, but with his heart.

'I know you hate my world, so I've taken an indefinite sabbatical. And I've done some stupid pointless things in my past, and I want to make amends, so I've set up a foundation for kids with special needs and I want you to help me run it. You and me.'

She stepped back, placing her palm between them. 'Whoa, not so fast. You've taken a sabbatical?'

'Time off, just to—well—to spend time with you and hopefully run a charity in Marshall's memory. In London.'

She smiled again. 'Gosh, really? That's such a wonderful thing to do. And I'd be honoured to help. But—'

'I do have some commitments I have to keep. The occasional dinner, a couple of small gigs. They won't take me away for long. And I'll be back. Straight away.'

The smile slipped. 'So I won't even be invited to these events?'

'Do you want to be?'

'I'd like to give it a try. It is only fair that if you step into my world, I step into yours.' Her brows lifted. 'I'm sure a girl could get used to designer dresses, fancy shoes and fine champagne, given time.'

'Then you'll be with me every step of the way. By my

side. Whatever you want. Anything.' He took her hand and held it against his chest.

'Anything?' A glimmer of a coy smile flitted back over her lips, a spark of light in her eyes, her hands tiptoeing up his shirt. 'So, I have a new bucket list.'

'Of course you have.' He felt the smile start from his heart and spread upwards. 'Does it include kissing a famous but hapless rock star backstage at the Manchester Globe Theatre?'

'It could.' As she pressed her lips against his he took the chance to tell her how he felt through his kiss. Just in case she missed his point. *I love you.* She stepped back breathless and flustered. 'Check.'

God, she was beautiful. 'Excellent. I could grow to really like lists. How about falling in love with a famous but hapless rock star?'

She nodded, hesitantly at first, then more confidently. 'Yes. Definitely. Very definitely. Head over heels.'

'Even more excellent.' He was on a roll, so he had to strike while the girl was hot. 'And I don't suppose it could also include marrying that same famous but hapless rock star?'

'Hmm. You're not exactly marriage material. You're an impulsive nomad who runs at the first whiff of commitment.' But she didn't let go of his hand. 'Lucky for you that's exactly the kind of guy I'm looking for.'

'So is that a yes? You'll marry me?' He whipped her into his arms, vowing silently never to let her go again.

She wound her hands round his neck. 'Was that what you LA people call a proposal?'

'I guess. Yes. Yes, it was. Marry me?'

'Hmm. I don't know…' But her long slow smile gave him the answer he'd been hoping for. Then her long slow kiss confirmed it. She was his. For ever. When she pulled back she bit her lip and wriggled her hips against his. 'But you'll have to do some serious work to convince me.'

'As long as it takes, sweet thing.' *For ever.* 'That's the bit I'm looking forward to the most.'

* * * * *

THE WEDDING SEASON
Concludes this month with Marnie's story in
Last Groom Standing by Kimberly Lang

Don't miss Reese's and Cassie's stories, out last month!

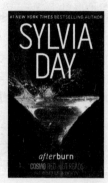

Come home this Christmas to Fiona Harper

From the author of *Kiss Me Under the Mistletoe* comes a
Christmas tale of family and fun. Two sisters are ready
to swap their Christmases—the busy super-mum, Juliet,
getting the chance to escape it all on an exotic Christmas
getaway, whilst her glamorous work-obsessed sister,
Gemma, is plunged headfirst into the family Christmas
she always thought she'd hate.

www.millsandboon.co.uk